THE
MIDNIGHT
LIBRARY

—

THE DEADLY CATCH

DAMIEN GRAVES

SCHOLASTIC INC.

New York   Toronto   London   Auckland   Sydney
Mexico City   New Delhi   Hong Kong   Buenos Aires

SPECIAL THANKS TO
ALLAN FREWIN JONES

—

ISBN-13: 978-0-439-89395-4
ISBN-10: 0-439-89395-X

Series created by Working Partners Ltd.
Text copyright © 2006 by Working Partners Ltd.
Interior illustrations copyright © 2006 by David McDougall

12 11 10 9 8 7 6 5 4 3 2 1   8 9 10 11 12 13/0

Printed in the U.S.A.
First printing, February 2008

Welcome, reader.

My name is Damien Graves,
curator of that secret
institution:

The Midnight Library.

Where is The Midnight Library, you ask?
Why have you never heard of it?
For the sake of your own safety, these questions are better left
unanswered. However . . . as long as you promise not to reveal
where you heard the following (no matter who or *what*
demands it of you), I will reveal what I
keep here in my ancient vaults.
After many years of searching,
I have gathered the most terrifying
collection of stories known to
humanity. They will chill you to
your very core, and make
the flesh creep on your young,
brittle bones. So go ahead, brave
soul. Turn the page. After all, what's
the worst that could happen . . . ?

Damien Graves

COLLECT ALL EIGHT SPINE-CHILLING VOLUMES IN THE MIDNIGHT LIBRARY.

—

VOICES

BLOOD AND SAND

END GAME

THE CAT LADY

LIAR

SHUT YOUR MOUTH

I CAN SEE YOU

THE DEADLY CATCH

THE
MIDNIGHT LIBRARY:
VOLUME VIII

Stories by Allan Frewin Jones

CONTENTS

THE DEADLY CATCH

"Mr. Fenton! Do you think we'll see any sharks in the bay?" Adam Walker called out from the backseat of the bus that was taking his class on a kayaking trip to the marina at Garner Bay.

His best friend, David Burns, was sitting next to him.

"Mr. Fenton!" David called. "If we see a shark, can we catch it and bring it back to school as a pet?"

Mr. Fenton turned and gave the two boys a weary smile.

"If you ask me, the only dangerous creatures out

there today are going to be you two," he said. "Now settle down, everyone. We're almost there."

Adam peered out of the windows of the bus. He couldn't wait to get out on the water. He loved kayaking and was becoming more confident, although David was much more experienced. But that was only because David's father and uncle often took him river kayaking on summer weekends. They had even been whitewater kayaking. Adam was secretly a little envious of David's ability, and he looked forward to the day when he was as good on the water as his friend.

The bus took a sharp turn to the left and began the long, steep plunge down to the bay. The road descended through a narrow gorge between grassy hillsides where sharp points of rock jutted out like broken bones.

Adam saw how Garner Bay formed a natural cove in the coastline of rugged, gray cliffs and weathered granite crevices. The modern-looking marina lay in a wide, sheltered harbor protected by thick seawalls that left only a narrow channel out into the open waters of the Atlantic. White foam boiled around the rocks that dotted the mouth of the cove. Beyond the cliffs, the ocean glittered beneath a cloudless blue sky.

"This is going to be a great day for kayaking!" Adam said.

"You bet it is!" David agreed.

The bus pulled up and everyone piled off, yelling and jostling as they squeezed out through the doors.

"Slowly! Slowly!" Mr. Fenton shouted above the noise. "Calm down! And stay by the bus, all of you. There's some stuff I want to tell you."

"Watch that door. You'll break it!" growled the bus driver as David and Adam joined the crowd near the exit. Adam grinned apologetically at the driver. But then he and David were sucked into the crowd clambering down the steps. A couple of hectic seconds later, they were spat out onto the asphalt.

The students spread out in the parking lot. Mr. Fenton called for quiet, but the nudging and pushing and laughing continued.

"Quiet, everyone!" Mr. Fenton bellowed. "Cut it out or we all go straight back to school!"

The elbowing and shoving stopped abruptly.

"That's better," Mr. Fenton said. "Let's keep it this

way. Now listen up. You can't go rushing around the marina like a gang of monkeys."

There were a few subdued gibbering noises, and David did a quick imitation of a gorilla beating its chest — until he was stopped dead by a mean look from Mr. Fenton.

"OK," Mr. Fenton said, gesturing toward the long, low glass-and-steel buildings of the marina. "In addition to welcoming school parties like ours, the Garner Bay Marina has facilities for yachting, surfing, windsurfing, and scuba diving — so I don't want you kids getting in anybody's way or making a nuisance of yourselves in any other way, got that?"

"What, *us*?" someone called, and there was some muffled laughter.

"There is also a fairly decent café where we will be having lunch if you behave yourselves," Mr. Fenton continued. "And we'll be touring the Garner Bay Museum of Local History and Nautical Sciences — which I'm sure you'll all find absolutely fascinating."

David yawned loudly behind his hand.

Mr. Fenton continued. "When we get to the kayaks, I want to make it perfectly clear that no one is to go out beyond the harbor walls."

There was a deep groan from David, which Mr. Fenton ignored.

"Out in the open sea, the currents can be very unpredictable," Mr. Fenton explained. "It's extremely dangerous. And in answer to Adam's question earlier on the bus, I have been told that at this time of year with the warm ocean currents coming up from the south, there have been a few sightings of mako sharks."

There was a general murmur of excitement. Adam looked at David.

"Wow, sharks!" he said. "I was only kidding when I asked about them."

Mr. Fenton held up his hand for quiet. "Makos can be very dangerous," he said. "So we're not going to take any chances."

"I'd know how to deal with a shark if I saw one," David called out. "I'd wait till it opened its mouth, then I'd jam my paddle between its jaws. That would stop it!"

"Or you could break your paddle in half, and then stab it in the eye with the broken end," Adam suggested. "It would go right into its brain and kill it."

"And what would you do if the shark had already bitten off both your arms?" Mr. Fenton asked in an amused voice.

"Then I'd head-butt it," David said confidently, bobbing his head sharply forward. "Right between the eyes!" Everyone laughed, and Adam saw that even Mr. Fenton had to smile at that one.

"Well, that's enough about sharks," he said. "OK, I know a few of you have had some experience with river kayaking, but controlling a kayak in the sea is very different — even in a sheltered harbor like this. That's why I've arranged for an instructor to give you all a lecture on safety as well as basic skills and techniques."

"When are we going to get into the kayaks?" someone asked.

"All in good time," Mr. Fenton said. "The lecture shouldn't take more than half an hour — so you'll have plenty of time on the water. Now follow me, everyone." Mr. Fenton turned and led the way through the glass entrance doors into the building.

"Half an hour?" David muttered. *"Bo-ring!"* He looked at Adam. "Let's just skip it," he said under his breath. "I probably know as much about kayaking as any dumb, old instructor."

Adam looked anxiously at their teacher. "I don't know," he said. "Old Fenton will go ballistic if we sneak off."

"He won't even notice we've gone," David insisted, hanging back as the others began to filter into the entrance lobby. "I'm going to check out the kayaks, even if you're not."

Adam hesitated at the door. David was already walking off down the side of the building.

"If we get detention for this, I'll strangle you," Adam muttered as he ran to catch up with his friend.

"You worry too much," David said with a glint in his eyes. "Think about it. Without Fenton and some lame instructor telling us what we can and can't do, we can go out of the harbor and finally have some fun!"

Adam frowned at his friend. "Is that such a good idea?"

David grinned widely. "It's a great idea," he said. He raised an eyebrow. "Of course, if you're too frightened . . ." His voice trailed off meaningfully.

That did it. Adam glared at him. "Let's go!" he said.

The boys had to keep out of sight around the side of the building for a minute or two until they were sure that there were no disapproving adults around. They didn't want anyone asking what they were doing. But once the coast was clear, they ran laughing toward the kayaks. They swiped life jackets and protective water-proof covers from an open shed by the waterside. They quickly put these on and then they picked out a couple of the best kayaks.

Adam stepped into his kayak and sat down carefully, one hand on the wooden dock as he felt the slim craft bobbing and shifting under him. It was all a matter of balance — of riding the gentle swell. He secured the waterproof cover onto the kayak and then cast off. He gripped the paddle in both hands and gave a good strong pull on the water, keeping the paddle vertical and holding the blade in tight to the side of the craft.

The kayak shot forward, and Adam smiled to himself. David was right — this was a million times better than a stuffy lecture.

"Hey, not so fast!" Adam called out. David was already several lengths ahead of him, paddling with long, smooth strokes, his kayak quickly approaching the gap in the seawall.

"Race you out of the harbor!" David called back.

A small voice spoke up in Adam's head: *You'll be in detention for a whole month if Old Fenton notices you've snuck off like this.* But Adam ignored it. He was already having too much fun to worry about Fenton.

He pulled on his paddle, working hard, trying to catch up with David. He noticed that the prow of his kayak was veering off the straight line. He corrected the drift with a good, swift pull — thrusting his paddle down into the water with the blade parallel to the keel and then pushing hard outward. The back of the kayak slid around in the water, and the prow moved back on course.

Adam called out to David. "And Old Fenton thinks we needed a beginners' guide to kayaking!"

"Yeah," David called back. "As if!"

The waves grew larger as Adam approached the mouth of the seawall, and the kayak rose and fell as he cut through them. Some of the larger waves even broke over the prow, but Adam had sealed everything tightly with the cover. There was no danger of water getting in. He felt a little uneasy for a moment as he struggled with the rising swell of the waves, but he managed to keep the kayak under control. Before long, his confidence began to soar again.

I can really do this! he thought. *Awesome!*

He followed David out into the open sea. They paddled to one side, moving out of sight of the marina. There were no other vessels out here, just the endlessly rolling waves.

David gave a whoop of joy as he turned his kayak into the path of a large, white-capped wave. Paddling strongly and confidently, he rode the wave, moving his body to keep balance as the light craft tipped and bobbed on the water.

Someday, I'll be able to do that, too, Adam thought as he watched his friend.

"Now you!" David called. Adam maneuvered his kayak to come up alongside the wave. Then the kayak dropped suddenly as it hit the trough. The sensation gave him a funny feeling in his stomach — queasy but somehow exciting. He felt the wave pick up the kayak and he did his best to keep the craft under control as he hit the crest. White water foamed all around him, and the kayak spun out of control. He leaned into the tilt of the kayak, stretching out his paddle and using the flat side of the blade to hold the kayak upright in the water. Cold water splashed his face, stinging his eyes. There was the taste of salt in his mouth.

The wave surged under him, but he kept his head. *Stay calm and keep going*, he thought. He quickly repositioned the paddle in an effort to steady himself as he rode the downside of the wave.

After a couple of frantic seconds, it was over. He let out a triumphant war whoop.

"Nice one!" David called, paddling nearby. "For a second there I thought you were going to tip over!"

"No way!" yelled Adam, spitting out seawater. "I can do anything you can do!"

David laughed. "In your dreams!" he said. "Try doing a roll! I'll show you how it's done, then you can try it." He paddled out to find a less turbulent stretch of sea. Adam chased him, glancing quickly over his shoulder — surprised to see how far away the seawalls already were.

"See any sharks?" David called out.

Adam scanned the water. "Nope," he said.

"Too bad! That would have been great!"

Adam nodded, but felt secretly relieved that the sea seemed to be empty of large predators — especially ones that could bite a kayak in half.

They were now out on relatively smooth water. David steadied his kayak. "Watch this!" he said. A moment later, he tipped over the kayak and vanished under the sea. Adam expected his friend to reappear right away — but the kayak stayed upside down, its long, slender keel washed by the waves.

A sudden unease grew in his chest. "David?" Adam called out. He dug his paddle into the water, speeding toward his friend's upended kayak.

A roll wasn't an especially difficult move — something must have gone very wrong.

Adam tried frantically to remember his training, but he had no idea what to do. The only option was to get out of the kayak and into the water. Maybe then Adam could help his friend.

He was just about to strip away the waterproof cover when he saw a sudden surge of movement from the kayak. It tilted onto its side, and there was a burst of white foam as David rose up, his hair plastered over his head, the paddle held firmly in his hands.

"How was that?" David asked. He was nearly breathless, and his whole body was dripping with water. "Impressive or what?"

"Not bad!" Adam said, swallowing his panic and stifling his desire to yell at David for scaring him like that. "But I've seen better."

"No way!" David shouted. "That was awesome and you know it. You try it!"

"Easy," Adam said. "Just watch this!"

He took a few long, deep breaths. Although he knew how to do a full roll, he had only tried it a few times in dead-calm river water.

He lifted his right knee and leaned out over the side of the kayak, keeping the paddle tight against his body. The kayak tipped, and he saw the water coming for him. He held his breath as he hit the cold water. He could see shafts of bright sunlight piercing the water through the swarm of bubbles. He used his hips and torso to complete the roll — reaching out the paddle in both hands, holding it flat, seeking the surface.

Once the blade broke the surface of water, he could use it to help lever himself up into the air again.

But as he twisted his body and dug at the water, he felt the kayak fighting him. It wouldn't turn. He struggled with the paddle, dragging it down to gain momentum — but still the kayak wouldn't move. Panic swept through him. He would have to get out of the kayak quickly, before he ran out of air.

But suddenly, the kayak responded to his movements. He came up out of the water, gasping and panting and spitting out salt water. David was laughing.

"You idiot!" Adam spluttered, realizing that it had been his friend who had been holding the kayak upside down in the water. "Why did you do that?"

But David just yelled with laughter and began to move away quickly along the coast.

"I'm going to squash you like a bug!" Adam shouted, setting off in the same direction.

"Yeah, yeah, yeah!" David called back. "You've got to catch me first!"

At first, Adam was concentrating so hard on catching his friend that he hardly noticed the thin wisps of sea fog that started creeping in all around them. It was the sudden cold that made him realize that something was going on. David was becoming less and less visible amid the fog, and the high cliffs were now a ghostly gray.

"Hey!" Adam shouted. "David — stop! We should go back!"

Even as he spoke, thicker tendrils of fog curled around his boat, wrapping him in the chilly air.

"Dav-id!" Adam called. His friend's kayak had vanished beneath the gray blanket.

"I'm here!" cried a faint voice. Adam peered into the mist. A small shape appeared. It was David, paddling toward him.

"Is this normal for this time of year?" David asked, staring into the dull, gray surroundings.

"How would I know?" Adam said. "We've got to get back."

"I know. Follow me."

David shot away. Adam tilted his hips, leaning the boat over and dipping his paddle in a series of wide "C" curves to turn it around. He followed David's stern, keeping close as the two of them paddled into the thickening fog.

They paddled side by side, their breath coming out in thick plumes. Neither of them was wearing a watch, so Adam had no idea how much time had passed while they had been trying to get back. He only knew that the outward journey hadn't taken this long.

"We should be back at the seawall by now," he announced. "Something's wrong."

"Idiot! I *know* something's wrong," David snapped back at him — and Adam was sure he heard a slight tremor in his friend's voice. He didn't like it — David was usually so confident. "I think we're lost," David said a few moments later. "I can't see a thing. For all I know we could be heading directly into the open sea."

"Oh, great!" Adam groaned. "Why do I always let you talk me into doing these stupid things?"

"This isn't my fault!" David said irritably. "I didn't put this fog here, did I?"

Adam felt something bump against his kayak. "What was that?" he said, his voice wavering a little.

"What was — *Oh!*" David let out a gasp. "Something just hit my kayak."

Adam stared into the murky water. He could see

something — thin, sinuous shapes, moving just under the surface of the water, circling the kayaks.

"They're sharks. . . ." he breathed.

"Don't be stupid," David said. "Sharks have dorsal fins. These are just ordinary fish." He beat at the surface of the water with the blade of his paddle. "Go away! Get lost!" he yelled.

The long, slender shapes glided downward and disappeared. If they were fish, then they were very long, skinny fish. Eels, possibly.

They paddled on side by side for a while longer. The chill air was biting into Adam's hands, and his fingers were beginning to feel numb. The waterproof covers kept him dry, but the cold was gnawing at his ears and nose. He couldn't remember ever feeling so wretched and miserable.

This had been *such* a bad idea!

"What if we really are heading out to sea?" Adam asked. "We might never be found."

"That's not going to happen," David said. "It won't be long before Old Fenton notices we're missing. He'll let the marina know, and they'll send out lifeboats to find us." He peered at Adam through the swirling fog. "It's not like we're going to stay lost out here forever!"

Adam frowned at him. "We'd better not," he said, trying to make a joke of it. "If we do, who's going to pester Old Fenton every day?"

They paddled on in silence for a while. Anxious thoughts tumbled through Adam's mind. What if the fog cleared and they found themselves adrift in the open sea with no sight of land? Then what would they do?

His thoughts were interrupted when something huge and white suddenly emerged out of the fog. The side of his kayak struck against a solid vertical surface.

Adam gasped in awe. He reached out a hand. The barrier felt smooth and hard. "It's a boat!" he shouted, relief flooding through him. But then he noticed an unpleasant smell — rancid and sour. It was like rotting seaweed, only worse. Much worse.

David came up close beside him. "What's that stench?" he asked. "Phew!" He shouted out. "Hey! Anyone up there? We're lost! Can you help us?"

The fog seemed to swallow his voice. There was no reply from the boat.

They both shouted together. "Help! He-e-elp!"

The only response was a muffled slap of waves on the white hull and a faint rhythmic creaking as the vessel rocked gently on the water.

"Are they all deaf up there?" asked David. "Hold me steady — I'm going to get on board."

David undid the waterproof cover and stood up carefully while Adam leaned over and held his kayak level.

"That's better," David said, his head and shoulders already half obscured by the thick fog. "We're at the front of the boat. It curves around, and I can feel a sharp edge." He called out. "Hey — anyone home?" There was no response. "I can see the top of the hull," David called down. "There's a rail. It feels a little slippery, but I think I can use it to pull myself up."

A few moments later, Adam heard David grunting with exertion as his legs lifted up into the fog. His feet kicked and scrabbled for a second or two before they were swallowed up in the grayness.

"Toss me the mooring rope," said David. "We don't want our kayaks drifting off. Then you climb up, too. There's slimy stuff all over the place, so be careful."

David reached down and took both mooring ropes from Adam. Keeping his hands on the boat, Adam stood up. The kayak wobbled suddenly, and he took a moment to regain his balance. The deck of the boat was at eye level. There was a chrome handrail to grasp as he hoisted himself onto the deck. David grabbed him under his arms to help him up.

"Well, at least we're no longer stuck in those tiny kayaks," David said as he tied the two ropes around the rail. He peered into the mist. "Where is everybody, though?"

Apart from the subdued slap of waves on the hull, Adam was aware of a dead silence all around him. It was almost creepy.

But now that he was on the deck, he was able to get a better idea of the boat. It looked brand-new, with gleaming white surfaces and chrome rails and fittings. But there was a kind of viscous, greenish-gray slime coating the deck. It dripped thickly off the rails. The awful smell was even stronger up here.

"What is this stuff?" David asked, rubbing his hands on his life jacket to get rid of the sticky substance. "Yuck, it feels like snot — and it really stinks."

As far as Adam could make out through the fog, the boat had two levels, a lower one with broad windows, and another smaller level on top — the bridge, he assumed — from which the boat could be steered.

The silence was oppressive. Adam shivered and clutched his arms around himself as the two friends stood on the gently rocking deck.

"The people on board must be as deaf as signposts!" David said loudly, as if he needed to break the silence. "Let's go and give them a surprise!" Adam could tell that David was trying a little too hard to make it sound as if everything was OK.

There was a narrow walkway that followed the curve of the hull. David went first. Adam followed, shuffling along carefully and holding on to a guardrail at shoulder height. The slime was slippery underfoot. He didn't want to lose his footing and end up in the sea.

The narrow walkway led to a lower deck and a doorway into the cabin. As Adam jumped down to follow his friend, his foot struck against something that was lying on the deck. He stooped and picked it up.

"Look at this!" he gasped. "It's a harpoon gun!"

David gazed at it. "Wow! And it's loaded, too." They could both see the thin metal arrow with a vicious-looking barb protruding from the barrel of the gun.

"That is wicked," Adam said. "I wonder if it works?"

"One way to find out." David snatched the gun out of his hands and in one quick movement aimed out over the side of the boat and jerked the trigger. There was a sharp hiss as the dart went speeding out through the fog. "Woo-hoo!" David said. "Did you see that?"

A moment later, they heard a dull thud — as if the arrow had hit something solid. The deck rolled under their feet as an angry wave slapped the boat. Adam and David staggered, both of them staring in confusion into the fog.

The boat became still again.

"What did you hit?" Adam breathed.

"I don't know," David replied. "A rock, maybe?"

They stood together, staring uneasily into the fog for a few moments.

Then David shook his head. "Come on — let's see what's inside." He climbed down into the cabin. As Adam turned to follow him, he was vaguely aware of a bulky shape behind them — but he couldn't make it out. Rather than cross the deck to investigate, he scrambled to follow David down into the cabin. No way did he want to be left up here on his own!

The fog had penetrated into the cabin, but it was much less dense. David managed to locate a switch, and he turned on the lights. Adam gazed around at the interior of the boat. There was a narrow table, padded benches, wooden cabinets, and even a small galley space.

The nasty smell wasn't so bad down here, and apart from some slithery smears of slime on the top steps, the cabin was clean and orderly.

But it was totally deserted.

"Where did everyone go?" Adam asked.

"Maybe the motor stopped working and the entire crew rowed off in a dinghy," David suggested. He stooped and pulled open a door.

Adam peered into the cabin from behind David.

"What's that noise?" he asked. As they stepped into

the small room, Adam could distinctly hear the sound of water sloshing around on the floor.

"It's nothing," David said.

Adam frowned. He wasn't so sure about that — the noise was gradually getting louder. He spotted a hatch in the floor of the cabin. He knelt down, twisted the handle to open it, and jerked the hatch up. The noise was instantly much louder. He peered into the gloomy hole. Moving water glistened in the light.

"I don't like the look of this," he said. "There shouldn't be this much water in here. Even I know that."

David knelt down at his side and stared into the hole. "I can see machinery under the water," he said. He looked at Adam with sudden alarm. "That's the engine," he said. "The boat must have a hole in it."

"You mean we're going to sink?" Adam said.

David nodded. "We need to get back to the kay-aks. Now!"

The water bubbled and foamed, rising toward the hatch.

The two boys wasted no time getting out of the cabin and edging back along the walkway to the prow. Adam tried his best to control his fear, but the thought

24

of being sucked down with the sinking boat was terrifying. His heart was beating fast as he followed David back to where they had tied up their kayaks.

David was crouching by the rail, holding a slimed mooring rope in his hand.

"What's wrong?" Adam asked.

David looked up at him, and the alarm in his eyes made Adam's heart skip a beat. David lifted the rope. The end dangled loose in the air.

"The kayaks!" Adam gasped.

"They're both gone," David said dully, as if he couldn't quite believe it. Adam noticed that the ropes were covered in slime.

"How did they come untied like that?"

"Maybe the sea pulled them loose," David said hesitantly, not sounding at all convinced.

Adam leaned over the rail. "Hey!" he shouted at the top of his lungs. "Is there anybody out there?"

The fog engulfed his voice. There was no answer.

"There has to be a radio on board," David said, getting to his feet. "It'll be on the bridge. We can use it to call for help."

They edged their way to the back of the boat again.

As he followed his friend, Adam's shoe slipped on the slime. It was a terrifying moment, but fortunately he was holding the rail and he quickly managed to regain his footing.

David looked around at him. "You all right?"

Adam nodded.

They came down onto the deck again. There was a short ladder attached to the bulkhead leading up to the bridge. David began to climb into the fog. Adam stood on the deck, squinting blindly in the direction of his friend.

"David?" he called. There was no reply. Adam frowned. A sudden panic struck him, and he scrambled up the ladder.

David was standing stiffly in the middle of the bridge, staring at something that captured all his attention. He didn't even seem to be aware that Adam was standing behind him. Adam followed the line of his friend's eyes. A chair faced the wheel at the front of the bridge — and slumped in it was a man.

"I think he's dead," David whispered in a cracked voice.

Adam swallowed hard, fighting a rising panic that

twisted his stomach into painful knots. He took a couple of long, slow breaths, trying to calm himself down. The fear subsided a little. David might be overreacting — maybe the man wasn't dead.

"We should make sure," Adam murmured.

"No way!" David protested. "I'm not going anywhere near him."

"We *have* to," Adam said. He gritted his teeth. Slowly, he walked across to the slumped man. The head was lying on the wheel, the face turned toward the two boys.

Adam bit his lip. The man's eyes were wide open, and his face was twisted in an expression of pain and terror. Across his cheeks and forehead and around his neck, Adam saw rows of purple bruises. The smell clogged Adam's throat and made him retch. It was that same rancid, rotting stench as before — only much worse. Slime dripped slowly from the man's clothes and his matted hair. Adam took a step backward, his feet slipping on the slick floor. He put his hand over his mouth and nose to try to keep out the smell.

"Well?" David called out. "He is dead, isn't he?"

"Yes." Adam's voice was just a croak.

"I knew it!" David groaned. "What do you think happened? Did he have a heart attack or something?"

"I don't know," Adam said. "The smell's really bad in here, and he's covered in that slime."

"How long has he been like that?" David asked.

Adam stared around at his friend. "What are you asking me for?" he said. "How should I know?"

The boat made a sudden surge on the water, and the man slid heavily out of the chair and landed facedown on the floor with a wet thud.

Adam let out a gasp of fear and backed away from the man. His feet slipped on the slime-coated floor, and he had to grab a rail to stay upright.

"This is bad," David said, slowly shaking his head. "This is really bad."

Adam stared around the bridge, forcing himself to stay calm. "What would the radio look like?" he asked. He turned and grabbed at David's collar. "Help me find it."

David stared into his friend's eyes, his breath coming in quick, short gasps.

"David!"

David pointed across the bridge. "That's the radio," he said, gesturing toward a black device with a microphone hanging on one side.

"Do you know how to use it?" Adam asked.

"I think so," David said hesitantly. "My uncle's boat has the same type of radio."

"Then do it!" Adam pushed his friend toward the radio. David stumbled the few paces across the bridge, his feet skidding under him on the slime. He stared at the device for a few seconds, then flipped a couple of switches. A crackling sound filled the air. He picked up the microphone and pressed a button on its side.

"Mayday! Mayday!" he shouted into the microphone. "We're on a boat off Garner Bay. There's someone dead here — and the boat is sinking. We need help." He released the button, and the crackling burst out again.

"Well?" Adam asked. "Is it working?"

"I don't know." David shouted the same frantic message into the microphone. There was another burst of meaningless noise but no response.

"Try again!" Adam insisted.

David shook his head. "I'm not staying up here with *that*," he said, glancing at the dead man. "Maybe there'll be a dinghy tied on behind — or an inflatable raft somewhere." He ran for the ladder.

Adam hesitated. Was it wise to give up on the radio so soon? Someone *must* have heard them. Adam tried one last time — nothing. Reluctantly, he turned to abandon the radio and help David look for other options.

But as Adam stepped out of the bridge, the air was pierced by the sound of a long, low siren.

He froze, staring into the fog and listening intently.

The siren let out a second blast. It sounded closer this time, and now he could see a bright cone of light scanning through the fog.

David ran to the side of the boat and yelled into the wall of grayness. "We're over here!"

Relief flooded through Adam. He joined his friend at the side and added his voice to David's wild shouts.

"Hey! Help! Over here!"

The siren blared out a third time, and the cone of

light came to rest on their boat. Adam saw a tall, narrow shape looming through the fog. A ship, approaching rapidly. As it got closer and emerged from the fog, he saw that it was a lifeboat.

"Hello there!" called a man's voice. "We were nearby. We got a distress call. Was it you? Are you in trouble?"

"Yes!" they both yelled.

The lifeboat turned sharply and slowed, moving closer and closer. It was larger than the fishing boat. It had a dark blue hull and a high orange super-structure that towered above them, bristling with antennae and other high-tech equipment. Men in bright-orange life jackets leaned out over the rails toward them. Adam had never felt so utterly relieved in his entire life.

There was the dull thud of an impact as the lifeboat's hull knocked against the fishing boat.

David scrambled to the rail. A man reached out and hauled him onto the lifeboat in a flurry of arms and legs. Adam was close behind. He stepped up onto the slippery rail and held his arms out toward his res-cuers. The boats dipped in the swell and moved a little apart. Adam found himself staring down into the gulf between the two hulls, where turbulent water foamed and seethed.

"Reach out!" one of the men called. "We'll get you!"

Adam leaned forward, and two men grabbed his arms. A moment later, the boats were pulled apart again. Adam let out a yell of fear as he was yanked off his feet and his legs were dragged over the rail. He dangled helplessly over the sea, kicking uselessly at the smooth hull of the lifeboat.

But the danger only lasted for a heartbeat or two. The two men pulled him up and over the lifeboat's rail, and he found himself standing, dazed and dizzy, on the deck. He felt a little battered and bruised by the frantic rescue, but he didn't care about that. The nightmare was over. They were safe now.

"Are you both OK?" one of the men asked. "There's a bad smell off that boat of yours. What happened?"

"We don't know," David said while Adam was still gasping for breath. "There's a dead person on there."

"Dead?" one of the men said sharply. "Dead how?"

Adam shivered. "I don't know, but he's covered in slime," he said.

The men stared at him.

"We were kayaking," David gabbled. "We got lost in the fog. We found the boat — we didn't think anyone was on board — then we found the dead man."

"And the boat is sinking, you say?" asked another man.

"I think so," Adam said. "We lifted the hatch in the cabin floor, and it looked like the engine was already covered in water."

There was a sudden powerful surge on the sea. The lifeboat was sent rolling from side to side. Adam clutched at a rail to steady himself as the deck tipped under his feet.

"What in heaven's name was that?" one of the men gasped as the lifeboat righted itself.

"I don't know," said the captain. "OK, that's it. I don't like this. Let's get back to shore."

The lifeboat made a sharp turn, and Adam heard the sound of the motor revving as they began to cut a rapid path through the fog.

"Here you go, boys," said one of the men, handing David and Adam steaming mugs of cocoa. "That'll take some of the chill out of your bones."

They huddled together, sipping the hot cocoa. Adam curled both hands around the hot mug, enjoying the heat on his skin.

"You two must have had quite a shock back there," the man said. "But don't worry. You'll be back on solid ground soon." The man was about to say something else when the boat began to rock again.

"You boys keep a tight hold of the rail," the man said. "It looks like we've come into another rough patch." He walked off along the deck, holding on to the rail with one hand.

Adam stared uneasily into the fog. He lifted his head, suddenly aware of a faint but familiar smell.

They both clung to the rail as the rocking of the boat got more severe. Suddenly, the lifeboat was pounded by huge waves. White foam cascaded high all around them, and the foul stench became so intense that Adam could hardly catch his breath.

He heard a man shout. He saw something long and thin whipping up out of the sea, lithe and sinuous as an eel. There was a deep, guttural roaring that seemed to fill the air all around them. And suddenly, the air was teeming with writhing green-gray tentacles — and on their whitish underside, Adam saw rows of suction discs.

Sticking out of one of the thrashing tentacles, Adam saw a harpoon — the same one that David had shot into the fog. Maybe that explained why the creature — whatever it was — sounded so angry.

Adam let out a yell as one of the tentacles curled around David's waist. Screaming and struggling, his friend was plucked bodily from the deck. He hung for a few seconds in the spray-filled air, then — with a dreadful rush — he was drawn down into the thrashing ocean. His screams stopped abruptly.

Adam clung to a rail and leaned dangerously far out to try to spot his friend in the sea.

"David!"

But there was no sign of him.

Even as Adam tried to grasp the dreadful reality of what had just happened, the sea boiled and another tentacle surged up in a spout of foam and came flickering toward him. The ghastly red sucker discs filled his vision. Adam let out a scream of sheer terror.

More tentacles filled the air, spraying water and slime as they lashed through the fog and came crashing down to grip the boat in a deadly embrace.

Adam reeled away from the stench, staring in disbelief as the boat tipped, dragged over by the clutching tentacles. He heard men shouting and screaming. The deck pitched under him, and Adam was thrown over the rail. He instantly felt the bite of icy water. He struggled in the seething sea, desperately trying to swim away from the capsizing boat. He saw men falling into the water. White foam spouted. The sea rose in a gushing fountain and, with terrifying speed, the lifeboat was dragged down below the waves.

A bellowing noise filled Adam's ears. He turned, his arms thrashing through the surging waves. The chaos and destruction seemed to continue in all directions, but if he swam as fast as he could, he might still escape.

Don't look back! Adam told himself. *Just keep swimming!*

He felt something rub against his shoulder.

"No!" he screamed.

Adam clutched on to some debris and tried to pry himself away from the unseen thing in the water.

"Adam," whispered the familiar voice of David, sitting atop a floating remnant of the boat's hull. "It was only me."

"You're safe!" Adam shouted.

"Shh! It will hear you."

David was shivering and covered in slime — but he was alive. He reached out his hand so that Adam could climb aboard the makeshift raft. Although the slime made it difficult to keep a firm grip, Adam managed to hoist himself out of the water within a few moments.

Then he noticed a pale, expressionless look on his friend's face.

"Your ankle . . ." David said in a low voice.

Adam kicked out, but the tentacle quickly coiled around his entire leg and pulled him back into the frigid sea.

The creature had caught him.

THE TRAP

Look, Crystal, we're home at last — and we've got a brand-new roof!" said Katie Herbert as her father brought the car to a halt outside their house. Katie stroked her beloved, golden brown cat through the bars of the wicker carrier. Crystal meowed plaintively and scratched to be let out.

Katie and her parents had been on vacation for the past two weeks. During that time, Crystal had been living with Katie's Aunt Julie. Even though Katie had loved every moment of their trip, she had missed her pet — and it was nice to be back home again.

"I hope the roofers have done everything I told them to do," Katie's father said.

"Don't start fussing, Ben," replied her mother. "They were very highly recommended."

"Regardless," he said, "I'd better check it out. Those new tiles are much heavier than the old ones, and the workers were told to put lots of wooden beams up there to help support the extra weight."

The family trip had been organized to coincide with the arrival of the roofers. Before the renovations, the weather-beaten roof had been dull and gray for as long as Katie could remember, but now it was made of warm red tiles. Katie thought they made the house look very cozy and inviting.

She unhooked the door to the cat carrier and pushed open the car door. "Off you go, Crystal." The cat made a long leap out onto the pavement. She jumped over the low stone wall and ran up the front path. Then she sat quietly on the doorstep, grooming herself, and waited for someone to let her into the house.

Katie climbed out of the car and stretched. She couldn't wait to call all of her friends.

But there was a lot of unpacking to be done first.

Katie ran up the path and opened the front door. She was hit by a peculiar, unfamiliar smell. It wasn't particularly unpleasant — just a little stale and musty. She stood in the doorway, sniffing. Her mom and dad came up the path behind her, carrying several large suitcases and bags behind them.

"Any chance of some help?" Katie's dad asked, half jokingly. Katie took her backpack out of his hand, heaving it up over her own shoulder. Crystal zipped into the hallway, almost tripping Katie's dad as he put down the rest of the bags. She sniffed the carpet, her whiskers quivering, then moved in a zigzag along the hall, her body low to the floor. It reminded Katie of how she stalked birds in the garden. Like she was hunting something.

Crystal streaked past the stairs and vanished into the kitchen.

"That cat is completely crazy," Katie's mom said, dumping more bags in the hall. She straightened up, sniffing. "What's that smell?"

"I don't know," Katie said.

Katie's dad joined them. "It's probably because the house needs to be aired out," he said. "I think I'll just go and check the roof, if you two can finish unpacking the car."

"No you don't," said Mrs. Herbert. "I want you to go down to the supermarket — we need some stuff for dinner." She smiled at him. "I've even made a list for you — just a few things."

"Why couldn't we have picked all this up on the way home?" he asked, eyeing the long list.

"Because there wouldn't have been room for it in the car," Mrs. Herbert pointed out. "You head for the supermarket, and Katie and I will get things organized here."

"Yes, ma'am!" Katie's dad said, giving his wife a salute and winking at Katie.

"Get out of here!" laughed Mrs. Herbert.

"And bring back something special for Crystal," Katie said. "She deserves some treats!"

"Will do," replied her dad, lugging the last few cases out of the trunk of the car. He climbed in behind the wheel and drove off with a cheerful wave.

Katie waved back to him from the front doorway. Then she picked up her backpack and began to heave it up the stairs to her room.

"I'll put on the kettle," her mom said, heading for the kitchen. "I'm in the mood for a nice cup of tea."

Katie was about halfway up the stairs when she heard the shriek. She propped the backpack against the banister and ran back down.

"Mom?" she called. "What's wrong?"

She raced into the kitchen. Her mom was pressed against the wall with a terrified look on her face. She was staring at something on the other side of the kitchen.

"What *is* it?" Katie asked, alarmed by her mother's expression of sheer panic.

"M-m-mice," her mother stammered.

Mrs. Herbert was looking at a cabinet beneath the countertop. The bottom corner of one of the cabinet doors had a triangular chunk missing. There was spilled sugar on the tiled floor and a scattering of small black beads. Mouse droppings!

"I *hate* mice," Katie's mother hissed with widening eyes. "I really hate them."

Katie noticed that Crystal had stationed herself in a low crouch right in front of the fridge. She was staring at the gap underneath it with her whiskers and ears at the alert.

"I suppose that explains the smell," Katie said. She walked calmly over to the cabinet. She crouched and opened the gnawed door. It was a terrible mess inside. The sugar bag had been nibbled away so that most of the sugar had spilled out. But that wasn't all — a bag of flour had also been chewed through, as well as two cereal boxes and a package of cookies. As she examined the spoiled food, Katie also saw a lot more mouse droppings and tiny mouse footprints in the scattered flour.

"They've been eating the Cheerios," Katie said, frowning. "Yuck!" She wasn't scared of mice, but she didn't like the idea of them snacking on her favorite cereal and spreading germs. That wasn't nice at all.

"Can you see any of them?" Her mom's voice trembled as she spoke.

Katie shifted the boxes and packages around, peering into the cabinet. She saw another gnaw hole in the back, but there were no mice in there now.

"I think we must have scared them off," she said, looking back up at her mom. She smiled reassuringly. "Don't panic. Crystal will get them if they show their faces in here again."

"Don't panic," her mother murmured, edging to the kitchen door. "Don't panic. Don't panic." Katie watched her mom draw a big breath. She walked out into the hall, her chin held high and her hands clenched.

Katie smiled a little. She sympathized with her mom's dread of mice, but all the same, it was a pretty extreme reaction to such small creatures. Katie opened the door under the sink and took out the dustpan and broom.

"You get 'em, Crystal," she said to the watchful cat as she began to sweep up the spilled food and the droppings. She got a garbage bag and filled it with the ruined items. Then she swept the bottom of the cabinet, squirted a damp cloth with some cleaning liquid, and scrubbed the area thoroughly.

All that time, Crystal remained crouching in front of the fridge, staring intently at the gap.

"I think Mom should see someone about her fear

of mice," Katie said to her pet as she pulled the ties tight on the garbage bag. "I mean, OK, they're messy and totally unhygienic, but what harm can they really do?"

She stood up and pulled her cell phone out of her jacket pocket. "Dad's going to have to get a few extra things — a new box of Cheerios, for a start." She speed-dialed her dad, holding the phone to her ear as she picked up the garbage bag and headed outside to leave it for the trash collectors.

The call went directly to voice mail. *He must be talking to someone else*, Katie thought. About ten seconds later, she found out who. Mrs. Herbert was sitting on the front doorstep with her cell phone to her ear.

"I'm not kidding, Ben," she was saying. "The place is infested! Either we get some exterminators in here *pronto*, or I'm out of here! No, I'm *not* overreacting — there were mouse droppings everywhere."

Katie stepped past her mom. Mrs. Herbert held the phone up to her. "Tell him, Katie!"

"It's true!" Katie called into the phone. "It was poo city in there! And we need sugar and flour and

Cheerios and whatever other cereal you like — the mice ate all of it!"

"See?" her mom said into the phone. "I'm calling the exterminators, Ben! No arguments!"

Chuckling at her mom, Katie dumped the bag in the garbage bin.

When she came back, her mom was still sitting there — but she was no longer on the phone.

"You OK?" Katie asked.

Her mom looked up at her. "I know you and your dad think it's really funny that I get so freaked out by mice," she said. "But just the thought of those little claws and beady eyes and twitchy whiskers — and the way they scamper in every direction." She shuddered. "Horrible, horrible things!"

"But we're not going to have them killed, are we?" Katie said, perching on a suitcase next to her mom. "We can ask the exterminator to put down traps that just catch them without hurting them." She frowned. "I mean, it's not like they're *evil* or anything."

Her mother eyed her. "That's a matter of opinion," she said. "But yes," she relented. "If we can get rid of them without killing them, that's OK with me. Although you might find that Crystal has her own ideas about that if she manages to catch any."

Katie suddenly made an ugly face. "But isn't that natural?" she said. "It's not the same as *us* doing it."

"If you say so," her mother replied. "Look, I really don't care if the little monsters are given a free trip to Florida," she said. "Just get them *out of my house!*" She looked at Katie. "And in case you think this is a big joke, I want you to know that I'm not setting foot inside that kitchen again till every single mouse is gone." Her mother raised an eyebrow. "And that means you and your dad can do all the cooking and washing and cleaning up in there till further notice, got it?"

Katie nodded. "I get it," she said with a sigh. "Anyone would think the place was infested with snakes, not tiny little mice!"

"Snakes I could handle," her mother said. "Mice — never!" She stood up. "OK, let's get the rest of this stuff inside — then I'm searching the Internet for a twenty-four-hour exterminator."

"Poor little things," Katie mumbled under her breath. "They're only trying to stay alive!"

"Not in my kitchen, they're not!" said her mother.

Katie walked through the kitchen a few hours later and into the laundry room to put another load into the washing machine.

Katie and her dad had made dinner. Mrs. Herbert had been true to her word and had not been in the kitchen all afternoon. Meanwhile, Crystal was still crouching by the fridge, whiskers erect, ears angled forward, her eyes fixed on that small, dark gap between the bottom of the fridge and the linoleum floor.

Katie sat cross-legged on the floor on the opposite side of the kitchen and watched her pet in fascination. Crystal had been waiting there patiently for hours now.

"Kill them quickly if you catch any," Katie told her pet. "No playing with them or tormenting them, OK?"

Her mother's voice sounded from the other side of the kitchen door. "Katie? I'm leaving the dinner dishes out here. Be a sweetheart and put them in the sink for me, OK?"

Katie sighed. "Listen, Mom, I really don't think the M-I-C-E are even here anymore," she called over the quiet hum of the washing machine. "If you want my opinion, they packed their bags and left as soon as we arrived." She got up and walked over to the kitchen door. She opened it and saw her mother cowering in the hall. "And anyway," Katie continued, "they're not going to come out with Crystal on guard duty, are they? Not unless they're suicidal. You're perfectly safe. Trust me."

Her mother gave her a dubious look. "I guess so," she said reluctantly. Picking up the dishes and knives and forks, she stepped into the kitchen.

"See?" Katie said.

"Hmmm . . ." said her mom as she walked gingerly across the floor. She put the dishes in the dishwasher and turned to look at Katie.

"I think they're gone," Katie said. "Really."

There was a sudden flurry of activity by the fridge. Crystal pounced — but a small gray shape zipped past her, moving across the floor like a long-tailed bullet.

Katie let out a startled yelp as it disappeared under the oven.

Crystal darted after the mouse, all claws and teeth and whiskers.

At the same moment, another gray streak zipped along the back of the sink and disappeared down the side of the countertop.

With a yell, Katie's mom ran out of the kitchen, yanking the door shut behind her. Seconds later, Katie heard the hammering of her mom's feet up the stairs and the loud slam of her bedroom door.

"Or maybe they're still here. . . ." Katie said to the empty room.

First thing the next morning, Katie's dad pulled down the ladder from the attic and climbed up through the trapdoor to check that the roofers had done a good job. Katie followed him up. She wasn't especially interested in wooden beams, but she always got a small thrill out of climbing so high up in the house. In the light of the single bare bulb, she saw that there were a lot of new wooden beams attached to the inside of the roof. Her dad stood up and gave one of the big, hefty, shoulder-level beams a thump with his hand.

"Good workmanship," he said, looking at her. "These should last a lifetime. No need to worry about the roof caving in on you."

Katie rolled her eyes. "That's such a relief, Dad," she said wryly. "Worrying about the roof caving in keeps me awake nights."

"You goofball!" laughed her father.

As she climbed back down the ladder, Katie heard the front doorbell ring and the door being opened. "Thank heavens," she heard her mother say. "Am I glad to see you!"

"Dad!" Katie called up. "I think the exterminator has arrived."

The exterminator was a cheerful, round-faced young man who introduced himself as Harry. He wore light blue overalls and carried a large chrome case with him. He held the case up in front of him and pointed out the bright orange writing on the front of it:

VERMIN? TRY VERM-OUT!

HOUSEHOLD INFESTATIONS ELIMINATED — GUARANTEED!

"OK," he said, with a big beaming smile, "I'm told you've a mouse problem." He winked at Katie. "I'll soon send 'em packing, don't you worry. How wide-spread are they?"

"Just in the kitchen as far as we know," Katie's mom said, pointing along the hall. "We came back from vacation — and there they were."

Nodding, Harry picked up his case and headed for the kitchen. Katie trailed after him.

"We don't want you to kill them," she told him. "Just get rid of them." She called out through the kitchen door. "Correct, Mom?"

"Whatever!" her mom called back. "I'm going shopping with your Aunt Julie." The front door closed with a bang.

"My mom hates mice," Katie confided.

"People often do," Harry said. "All right — let's take a look at the problem."

Katie's dad came into the kitchen. "If my wife finds any trace of mice in here, I'll be doing the cooking for the next six months."

Harry chuckled. "No sweat," he said. "I'll get rid of 'em for you." He put his case on the floor and opened it, revealing all kinds of strange devices. He took out a flashlight, then crouched down and pulled the kick-plate off from under the cabinets. He shone the flashlight under there. "Wow," he said. "How long were you on vacation?"

"Two weeks," Katie told him. "Why?"

Harry knelt up. "Judging by the droppings under here, you've had an infestation in here for some time. This is the level of activity I usually find in a house that's been empty for six months or more. It's amazing! Come and look for yourself."

"I'll take your word for it," Mr. Herbert said, holding up his hands in protest. "The question is: Can you do something about them?"

Katie knelt down and looked under the cabinets. She could see that the floor was scattered with mouse droppings.

"Oh — yuck and double yuck!" Katie said, getting up and looking at her dad. "I don't think we should tell Mom how long they've been here," she said. "She'll need therapy!"

"Just leave them to me," Harry said. "I'll have this place cleared within the week — guaranteed."

"Can you do it without killing them?" Katie asked.

Harry nodded. "I can put down humane traps if you like," he explained. "They'll be captured alive, so they can be taken off somewhere else."

"That sounds good," Katie said.

Harry looked at her dad. "Of course, you can't let them out in the garden or anywhere nearby. They'll just find their way back again. Ideally, they should be taken to a big open area — a public park or out into the country."

Katie looked hopefully at her dad, but he was frowning.

"Not a chance, Katie," he said. "If you think I'm driving a bunch of mice out into the country to give them their freedom before I go to work every morning, you're crazy! I'm sorry, but those mice are going to have to die."

"Oh, *Da-ad* . . ." Katie said.

"It's not an option, Katie," her dad said, and she knew by his tone that this wasn't up for discussion. And if she was honest with herself, she could see his point of view. After all, there might be dozens of mice.

"How will they be killed?" Katie asked Harry. "Will it be quick and painless?"

Harry took a white plastic box out of his case. "Normally, we use these," he told her. "See the hole? The mice go in through there and eat poisoned bait. Then they go back to their nests and die."

"That's so cruel!" Katie said.

"It's not as cruel as other methods," Harry told her. "Some people mix dry plaster with flour as bait. The mice eat the mixture, and the plaster hardens inside their guts and kills 'em — imagine that!"

Katie gave him a horrified look.

"So there'll be a whole lot of dead mice under the floor, I suppose?" Mr. Herbert said. "What about the smell?"

"There won't be any," Harry said. "The bodies just mummify in the nests. It's perfectly hygienic."

"OK then," Mr. Herbert said. "We'll go with the poison."

"I'll just grab some boxes and a can of poison from the van," Harry said. "Is there a basement?"

Katie pointed to the basement door, opposite the kitchen door. "There's a big shelving unit at the bottom of the stairs," she told him. "We keep our spare food supplies down there."

Harry walked down the steps. He came up a minute or so later, reporting that he'd seen more signs of mice.

"Better put a few boxes of bait down there, too. Just to be on the safe side," he said.

"Will the poison do my cat any harm if she eats it?" Katie asked.

"Not in small doses," Harry said. "Anyway, it should be secure enough in the bait boxes. But I'd keep the refill cans out of your cat's reach, if I was you."

It took Harry about half an hour to set up all the poison boxes and to show Mr. Herbert how to open them and replace the eaten poison.

"OK then," he said, crouching on the floor and tapping the keyboard on his laptop. "I'll just give you your invoice for services rendered so far." There was a low buzz as the invoice was printed. "I'll be back in a couple of days, just to see how things are progressing. But I'd say we'll be done within the week — guaranteed."

Katie and her dad saw him out.

"Poor mice," Katie said as she closed the front door on him.

Her dad was standing there staring at the invoice with a shocked look on his face. "Poor mice?" he gasped. "Poor *us!*" He stared at Katie. "I hope he was right about getting this resolved in a week. These people are really expensive!"

Katie's mom was pleased to hear the good news when she got home later that afternoon. She staggered through the front door, carrying a big bag full of metal storage containers that she'd bought to stop the mice from getting into their food again.

"Are they only in the kitchen?" she asked. "Did he check anywhere else?"

"They'll only be where there's a food supply," promised Katie's dad. "Don't panic — they'll be gone within the week."

"Good!" Katie's mom said. "What's for dinner — and who's cooking it?"

Later that evening, Katie was curled up on the couch between her mom and dad. They were happily watching television when Crystal marched proudly into the living room and dropped a dead mouse on the carpet right in front of them.

Katie's mom let out a scream and disappeared around the back of the couch.

"Get it away from me!" she yelled.

Katie gently shooed Crystal away from the tiny gray corpse.

"She's only doing what comes naturally," Mr. Herbert said. "Don't scold her."

"I wasn't going to," Katie said. She stroked Crystal's head. "Such a clever girl," she said.

Mr. Herbert picked up the dead mouse by the tail.

"What are you going to do with it?" Katie asked.

"Toss it in the garbage," her father said.

"You can't do that," Katie said. "We have to give it a proper burial in the garden."

"I don't care what you do with it!" Mrs. Herbert shouted from behind the couch. "Get it out of here!"

Katie's father looked dubiously at his daughter. "In the garden?" he said.

Katie nodded solemnly. "In the flower bed," she said.

"Come on, it's not dark yet. I'll get a gardening shovel out of the shed."

Katie led her father out of the room. Crystal rubbed up against her legs as she walked, purring up a storm.

"Yes, yes," Katie said, leaning down to pet her again. "You're a good girl," she cooed. "But next time, can you avoid bringing them into the living room, please? Mom is going to have a heart attack otherwise!"

On Monday morning, Katie had to go back to school after the break. She and her dad agreed that she should make breakfast in the mornings, and he would prepare the evening meal. Each morning, she dreaded finding poisoned mice strewn about the floor. But she never saw a single one. Her mom's storage containers had pretty much cut off the food supply to the mice, and there were no more droppings to be seen.

Of course, the fact that Crystal was on sentry duty most of the time probably helped keep the mice at bay. Katie was often woken by Crystal meowing down by the side of her bed. There would be a dead mouse on the carpet.

"Thanks, Crystal," Katie would say, carefully

tiptoeing around each new offering. "Such a clever girl." She dealt with these gruesome gifts by wrapping them carefully in tissues and burying them in the garden.

Early on the third morning after Harry the exterminator's visit, Katie padded down to feed Crystal and to get breakfast ready.

As she opened the kitchen doorway, she froze. "What on earth . . . ?" She rubbed her eyes and looked again at the kitchen floor.

The poisoned bait boxes had been pushed together into the middle of the floor. All seven of them.

That's weird, Katie thought. *Why would Dad do that?* Harry had said that the boxes shouldn't be moved, so why were they all clustered together in the middle of the floor?

Katie walked in a slow circle around the pile of boxes. She decided it was best to leave them alone, just in case there was some good reason why her dad had moved them. Shaking her head, she unlocked the garden door and quickly buried today's dead mouse, digging a little grave for it near the wall with a small shovel she now kept there for that purpose.

Afterward, she came back indoors, fed Crystal, and started preparing breakfast.

Her dad came down a few minutes later, half dressed and with tousled hair.

He stared at the gathered bait boxes. "Katie?" he said. "What did you do that for? You know Harry said to leave them where they were."

She looked at him. "I didn't move them," she said. "I thought you did."

Her dad shook his head. "Why would I do that? They were all in their usual places when I went to bed."

"Maybe the mice did it," Katie said with a grin, "out of protest!"

"It must be that cat of yours," her dad said. "She spends most of her time in here nowadays. Crystal was probably hunting a mouse and knocked the boxes all over the place as she chased it, or she was playing a game, batting the boxes with her paws."

"Well, she needs to stop doing that," Katie said thoughtfully. "Maybe we could weigh down the boxes with something so she won't be able to move them." She looked at her dad. "Isn't Harry coming back today?" she said. "Who's staying home to let him in?"

"Your mom's taking a day off from work," her dad told her. He held up his hands — with his fingers crossed. "Let's hope he gives us some good news. I'm really looking forward to your mom's cooking again."

Katie arrived home after school that afternoon and went into the kitchen to get herself a drink. She looked around. The bait boxes were gone.

Fantastic! she thought. *The mouse problem must finally be over.*

She went back out into the hall. "Mo-om?" she called.

"Computer room," her mom called from upstairs.

Katie ran up there. The computer room was set up like a small office. It was a quiet place where her mom and dad could work — and where she could do her homework without distractions. Her mom was at the computer, typing.

"Are we mouse-free?" Katie asked eagerly. "Because I'd really like one of your special fajitas for dinner, if you're back on kitchen duty."

Her mother looked up from the monitor and gave

Katie a long look. "Do you want to know what our pal Harry had to say for himself?" she asked. Judging by the expression on her face, Katie got the feeling it wasn't going to be good news. "He said he couldn't understand it. There were freshly gnawed holes inside the kitchen cabinets, and just as many mouse droppings under there as before. His so-called poison doesn't seem to have made the slightest difference. The only reason there haven't been droppings all over the floor is because the mice are staying out of the cat's way."

Katie perched on the edge of the desk. "So, what's the plan now?"

"Harry's plan was to come back with a couple of friends and dismantle the kitchen. He was going to pull up some of the linoleum and rip out the shelving and take apart the cabinets to find the nests."

"You're kidding!" Katie said with a gasp. "You're not going to let him wreck the kitchen, are you?"

"No, I'm not," said her mom. "I'm not having my kitchen torn apart because of a bunch of mice. Not unless there's no other option." She gave a grim smile. "And fortunately there is. Do you remember us telling you that your great-grandfather used to run a store called The Ironmonger's Shop?"

Katie nodded. She remembered, because "ironmonger" was such an odd word. Her dad had explained it to her once. A long time ago in Europe, ironmongers' shops used to sell household goods — everything from screws and nails to pots and pans and paint and ladders and silver polish and brooms.

"Well, when the store was closed down, a lot of your great-grandad's stock was put away in a self-storage facility," her mom continued. "Your dad remembered that he used to sell those old-fashioned steel-spring mousetraps. He's going to swing by there on his way home this evening and see if the traps are still there. And if they are . . . then that's it for those mice!"

Katie had seen how those traps worked. A small piece of bait is placed on the wooden base, and the steel-spring trap is locked in position so that when a mouse steps on the plate — *bam!* Sometimes the mouse survives — and sometimes not.

Katie shuddered at the thought of the kinds of awful sights she was going to be seeing in the kitchen from now on.

———

Katie was in her room watching TV when she heard the toot of the car horn. She glanced out of the window. Her dad was standing at the open trunk of the car, beckoning up to her. She ran down the stairs and out onto the pavement.

"Did you get the traps?" she asked him.

"Take a look for yourself," he said. There was a big, old-fashioned brown suitcase in the trunk. Katie lifted the lid and saw what looked like several dozen wood-and-steel mousetraps in there.

"And take a look at this one," her dad said, opening the passenger door. He pulled out a huge mousetrap. It must have been more than a foot long. "I just brought it over to show you," he said. "I'd forgotten all about it. Your great-grandad had it made especially for a window display. I remember the sign he had over it: NO MATTER HOW BIG YOUR RODENT PROBLEM, WE'VE GOT THE RIGHT TRAP TO DEAL WITH IT." He tucked the huge trap under his arm. "OK, Katie, help me get this case into the house. The sooner we get these traps set up, the sooner we can get things back to normal."

Katie picked one of the traps out of the case. She pulled back the lethal steel spring and set it, holding the trap out on the flat of her hand. Her dad took a pen out of his shirt pocket and touched its end against the metal trigger. The steel bar snapped across so quickly that it made Katie jump. The end of the pen was caught hard and fast.

"Good night, mousie," her dad said.

"I don't think any of the mice are going to survive that," she said, looking at her dad. "It's cruel."

"Yes, it is," her father agreed. "And if you can come up with an alternative, I'm prepared to try it."

Katie chewed her lip, thinking hard. "No," she admitted at last. "I can't."

It didn't take long for the two of them to set the traps and scatter flour over the deadly metal plates. Within an hour, Katie and her dad had made the kitchen, the utility room, and the basement lethal places for a mouse to set foot.

Now it was time to eat. Katie's dad got the wok out while she started slicing vegetables into fine strips

67

ready for a stir-fry. Her mom was upstairs taking a shower.

"We're out of noodles up here," her dad said, his head in the cabinet. "Katie — be a sweetheart and get me some from the basement."

"Will do."

Katie opened the basement door and flicked the light switch.

The light didn't come on. She flicked the switch back and forth a few times.

"The bulb's out," she called. There was just enough natural light coming from the kitchen window for her to make her way down safely. Dad always kept a flashlight hanging from a nail at the bottom of the stairs by the big old shelving unit where their spare food supplies were kept.

Katie stepped down in the half-light. She lifted the flashlight strap off the nail and switched it on. The powerful white beam illuminated the basement's dusty, cobwebby brick walls and the dark, low rafters of the floor above — as well as all the old furniture and bric-a-brac and household items that were kept down there.

Katie reached for a package of noodles.

She gave a gasp and pulled back her hand. A small shape crouched on the shelf, caught in the beam of light. The red points of watchful eyes glinted in the light.

It was a mouse.

"You awful thing!" Katie said, recovering from the initial shock. She waved her hand at the mouse. "Shoo! Go away!"

The mouse didn't move. It just crouched there, staring straight at her with beady eyes the color of blood. And then Katie realized that there were more points of red light on the shelves. Many more.

Her heart began to beat fast as she inspected the shelving unit with the flashlight. On every shelf, perched on every can and package of food, and filling all the gaps between, were dozens and dozens of mice — all perfectly still, all crouched low, all staring straight at her with unblinking red eyes.

Katie's skin crawled and her mouth became dry. She wanted to shout out to her father, but her throat was too constricted. The beam of the flashlight shook as her hand began to tremble.

Mice don't do this, she thought. *This is* not *how mice behave*.

"No . . ." Katie's voice was little more than a whisper.

She groped blindly behind herself for the post at the bottom of the stairs, unable to tear away her eyes.

She lifted a foot and felt backward for the bottom step.

It was like a nightmare — a bad dream.

Very, very slowly — terrified that the whole silent army of mice would come surging toward her at any moment — Katie backed foot by foot, step by slow step, up the stairs.

Two steps from the top, she turned and threw herself up into the hallway. She slammed the door shut behind her and scrambled to her feet.

"Dad!" she yelled, running into the kitchen.

Her father stared at her. "Katie — you're as white as a sheet. What happened?"

"Mice!" Katie managed to say. "Hundreds of mice. Down there."

Her father's eyes narrowed. "Is that so?" he said, striding toward the basement.

Katie grabbed his arm. "No — don't," she said.

He looked at her. "Don't be silly," he said. "I want to see how many there are."

She looked imploringly into his face. "They're not normal mice, Dad. Please don't go down there."

"Shush now!" he said. He took the flashlight out of her hand. Katie shrank back as he opened the basement door, half expecting a filthy gray tide of mice to come pouring out over him.

He shone the flashlight down into the basement.

"Come on, mice — show yourselves," he said as he stomped down the stairs.

Katie's heart was beating so hard that she could hardly hear anything else. Any second now . . .

"Katie?"

"Can you see how many there are?" she called down.

"Come on down here," he called up.

Dragging her feet, she moved to the threshold of the stairwell. Her father was at the bottom of the steps. She could see the flashlight moving in every direction.

"Show me where you saw these mice," he called up to her. "I can't see a single one."

It took all of Katie's courage to make her way back

71

down those stairs. She felt almost faint with fright as she came down to where her father was standing. She looked at the shelving unit. There were no mice.

She let out a long, shuddering breath. She looked around the basement.

"They're gone," she murmured.

Her father grinned down at her. "How many did you see?" he asked.

"Dozens and dozens," Katie said.

He put his arm around her shoulders. "Now that's what we call the power of suggestion," he said.

She blinked at him. "Huh?"

"They were all in your mind," her father explained. "You came down here thinking about mice and expecting to see mice — and so you saw mice. But they were all in your head, Katie." He smiled down at her. "Don't worry about it. It can happen to the best of us." He crouched and picked a new lightbulb off the bottom shelf.

"They were real," she breathed. "They *were*. They were just sitting there staring at me. That was what was so weird about it."

Her dad handed her the flashlight and walked

along to where the dead bulb hung. He unscrewed it and replaced it with a new one. "Be a sweetheart and switch on the light," he said.

Katie walked slowly up the stairs. Could she really have imagined it? No, the mice had been real. She could still see those sharp, unblinking eyes in her mind. It couldn't have been a hallucination . . . and yet . . .

She flipped the light switch. Nothing happened.

"That's odd," her father said. "Hold on — I'll try another bulb."

Katie sat on the top step and waited while her father inserted another lightbulb. The light still didn't come on.

Her father strode up, looking annoyed. "This is beginning to make me angry," he said. "I bet those loathsome rodents have gnawed through the electric cable down there. That kind of thing could be really dangerous; it could start fires. If those traps don't do the trick and get rid of them in the next couple of days, we're going to have to get a hold of some professionals again. Harry wasn't very successful — maybe we should try someone else."

"So there *were* mice down there," Katie said. "I told you so. . . ."

She was cut short by a fearful scream from upstairs. *Mom!*

Her dad ran to the bottom of the stairs. "Alison? Are you OK?" The screaming didn't stop. He pounded up the stairs. Katie raced after him, terrified. She had never heard her mother sound so scared.

Her mom was huddled in a corner of the landing outside her open bedroom door. She was wearing nothing but a bath towel, and her hair was wrapped up in another towel.

"In there! In there!" she panted, her eyes wide.

Katie followed her dad into her parents' bedroom. The bottom drawer of her mom's dressing table was open, and some of her mom's socks were scattered on the carpet.

Katie's father made a revolted noise in his throat. Katie peered into the drawer. It was seething with dozens of mice.

Her dad shouted and kicked at the open drawer. There was a wild flurry of movement as the mice ran for cover, spilling out over the front and sides of the drawer and racing to find the safety of dark corners under the armoire and the bed.

"Oh, that's so disgusting," Katie said in a hushed voice, staring at the droppings and the torn, chewed-up pile of socks in the drawer.

"Katie?" Her mom's voice was slightly more controlled now.

Katie went to the door. "They're gone," she said.

"I don't care," her mom said. "Get me some clothes — nothing from that drawer!" She pulled the towel tight around herself. "I'm going to get dressed," she announced. "Then you're going to pack me a suitcase — and I'm going to stay with your Aunt Julie till every single mouse is gone from this house and the whole place has been cleaned from top to bottom." She glared at her husband. "And I don't care how much it costs."

She disappeared into the bathroom and slammed the door.

An hour later, Katie and her dad waved good-bye to her mom as she drove away from the house in Aunt Julie's car.

Her dad closed the front door. He looked

thoughtfully at her. "You sure you don't want to go with her?" he asked. "I can still drive you over there if you change your mind."

Katie shook her head. "I'm fine," she said.

"Super," her dad said. "All right — we've got some work to do. Those wretched vermin could be anywhere. I'll set some traps downstairs, and you can be in charge of the situation upstairs. Be sure to leave a trap in every room up there."

It took a while for the traps to be redistributed all over the house. Katie even placed one in her mom's sock drawer. *That will give those horrid things a terrible shock if they come back,* Katie thought.

Later in the evening, Mom phoned from Aunt Julie's house. Katie chatted with her until Dad came into the living room with two steaming plates of a very late stir-fry meal.

"There are traps absolutely everywhere," Katie reassured her mom. "Trust me — they'll get the message now for sure."

"I hope you're right," said her mom. "Well, I'll go now, sweetie. Sleep tight."

"You, too," Katie said, hoping she sounded calmer than she really felt. "I'm fine. Those mice don't scare me!"

Katie awoke suddenly from a bad dream. She stared up at her shadowy bedroom ceiling, trembling and sweating. She had been dreaming that she was very tiny, huddled up in the corner of a huge cabinet while gigantic red-eyed mice scrabbled and gnawed at the wood, trying to get at her.

Not much fun! She turned her head and saw that it was three o'clock. It was a weird time to be awake.

As she lay there, she became aware of noises. They were coming from the attic. Or at least, that's what it sounded like, although she was only half awake.

She listened more intently. Yes — there *were* noises from up there. Skittering, scrabbling noises, like tiny feet scampering all around. And other noises, too — faint but persistent gnawing and chewing noises, and occasionally the odd deep, brief creak.

So the mice were up in the attic now!

The thought of them scuttling around up there over her head gave her the creeps.

She began to regret her decision not to go with her mom.

What if the mice nibbled through her ceiling and came raining down on her in bed? She shuddered at the thought.

She pulled the covers up to her chin, arguing with herself as to whether she should go and wake her dad. She didn't want him to think she was being a coward — not so soon after she'd told him she was fine.

In the end, she decided to stay put. She turned over and pulled the covers up over her ears to try to block out the disturbing noises. It was a long time before she was finally able to get back to sleep, and even then her dreams were full of scrabbling claws and wicked, beady eyes.

Katie! Time to get up, sweetie!"

Katie woke with a start at her father's call and the cheerful *rat-tat-tat* of his knuckles on her bedroom door.

"OK!" she called back. "Coming."

The door was slightly ajar as always, allowing

Crystal to come and go. Katie leaned over the side of the bed and peered down at the carpet. She sighed. A small twisted gray form lay there. Another nocturnal gift from the cat.

She pulled tissues from the box at her bedside and carefully wrapped up the little body and put it on the edge of her bedside table.

A few minutes later, washed and dressed, she went downstairs, holding the little bundle of tissues in her hand. Her father was in the kitchen, on his knees with a plastic bag. He grinned up at her.

"I think we're on a roll here!" he said, lifting up a dead mouse by the tail before dropping it into the bag. "I found three upstairs and five so far down here. These traps are magnificent!"

Katie looked quickly away. "Great," she said uncomfortably. She spotted several traps that her dad had not yet emptied. The metal bars lay across the little bodies, almost cutting them in half. There was no blood or anything, but it was still pretty gruesome. She certainly didn't want to look at anything like this so early in the morning.

Katie quietly went out into the garden and buried

her own little mouse corpse. Then she returned to the kitchen and began preparing breakfast for two.

"I dreamed I was being chased by huge murderous mice last night," Katie said.

"That sounds terrible," her dad said. "Did they get you?"

"No, I woke up. Oh, I almost forgot — I think I heard them up in the attic, when I woke up in the middle of the night."

Her father sat up straight, a resigned look on his face. "Well, it wouldn't surprise me," he said. "The little devils are everywhere else. I guess I'd better put some traps up there, too." He looked at her, shaking his head. "Can you believe these mice? They've really made themselves at home."

Katie looked anxiously at him. "But we will get rid of them, right?"

He frowned. "I'll tell you what," he said. "We'll give it one more day, and if things don't seem to be getting any better, I'll call Harry back to do whatever it takes."

Katie nodded. "I think that's a very good idea," she said.

—

Mr. Herbert left work early that afternoon and drove Katie home from school. Back at the house, they found Crystal sitting proudly on the doormat, waiting for them with a dead mouse at her feet.

"We could use twenty more like her," Katie's dad commented. "Then we might start getting somewhere." He let them into the house. "OK — let's see what the tally is."

Katie refused to have anything to do with emptying the traps, but it did seem that they were being horribly effective. Her father kept count of the mangled bodies as he popped them into a plastic bag.

"Twenty-three!" he announced loudly, coming into the kitchen from a tour of the whole house. "That's a record."

"Great," she said, but privately she was beginning to wonder how many mice they would have to kill before they could reclaim their home.

"Tell you what," he said. "I've got some work to do. Could you make dinner for us tonight? I'll handle breakfast tomorrow in return, promise."

"Yes, that's fine," Katie said. "Will grilled ham and cheese sandwiches be OK?"

"Delicious," her father said, heading out of the kitchen. "Give me a call when they're ready. Oh, and I'd love a cup of coffee, if you have a minute."

"Will do."

Katie got to work. First, she took two thick slices of ciabatta and smeared them with butter. Then she topped the bread with ham and slices of cheese. She placed everything in the sandwich maker until the cheese melted. It was a Herbert family favorite.

Crystal came trotting into the kitchen.

"Your nose!" Katie said with a laugh. "You can smell ham two streets away, can't you?" Crystal meowed and stood up against the table leg.

"No, sorry, this isn't for you," Katie told her. She took the sandwich and a coffee up to her dad.

"How's it going?" she asked him.

"Horrible. End-of-the-month utility bills — I hate them."

"Never mind. Try this."

"It looks scrumptious," her dad said as she put the plate down next to him.

Or . . . you never know, Katie thought as she climbed into bed. *If she's feeling especially guilty, I might get two or three mice!* She gave a little shiver. *I'll be really glad when this is over*, she said to herself as she pulled the covers up around her ears. *Well, there don't seem to be any mice in here, at least.*

She switched off the bedside light and curled up under the comforter.

Katie's sleep was disturbed by a muffled cry, shrill but distant.

It was a terrible, penetrating sound that ended abruptly, full of agony and distress. A badly hurt animal, maybe? Cats fighting in the garden? Except Katie could have sworn the strange noise had come from inside the house — from somewhere downstairs. She listened sleepily for a few moments, but there were no more cries. Maybe she had imagined it.

It was probably just a dream.

In less than a minute, she was fast asleep again.

She was awoken again in the middle of the dark night by something furry brushing against her foot.

"Crystal, stop that," she mumbled. "Go away, girl. It's too early." She turned over under the comforter, pulling her foot away from the tickling fur.

Her toes dug into a mass of something that squirmed and moved — wriggling under and over her foot like dozens of hairy fingers crawling across her skin.

The shock forced her eyes wide open as she convulsively jerked her legs away from the writhing things.

For a moment, she thought she must be having another nightmare. But she wasn't asleep — she was horribly awake. She groped for the bedside light, drawing herself up into a huddle at the top of the bed.

She stared down at the comforter. Where her feet had been a moment before, the comforter was bulging and moving as if . . . as if there was something *alive* underneath.

Katie grasped the comforter in both hands and dragged it up from the end of the bed.

She let out an involuntary scream of fear and horror.

Dozens of mice were swarming over her mattress —

writing and squirming on her bedsheet in a disgusting mass of dirty gray bodies.

Realizing they were exposed, the jittery creatures scattered and poured down over the sides of her bed like torrents of filthy water.

"Dad!" Katie screamed, hurling the comforter off herself and scrambling out of bed. Her bare feet accidentally came down on squirming bodies. She felt little bones cracking under her weight. She heard thin, piercing squeals and piping screeches. Mice ran over her feet as she plunged toward her bedroom door. Teeth and claws dug like needles into her skin.

She threw her door open and tumbled out into the hallway — almost colliding with the loft ladder, which was jutting down from the open trapdoor in the ceiling.

Even in her shock and panic, she knew that the ladder had not been down when she had gone to bed. Her father must have been up there in the late evening — laying more traps, maybe?

Katie slammed her bedroom door shut behind her and fell to her knees on the hallway carpet, gasping for breath, her heart thundering against her rib cage, her stomach in knots.

Her parents' bedroom door flew open. Her father came running into the hall in his pajamas.

"Katie, what is it?" he gasped, his face heavy with disturbed sleep.

She fought for breath, pointing back to her room. "Mice . . . in my bed . . . everywhere . . . horrible . . . horrible . . ." she panted.

Her father switched on the hall light. Katie was relieved to see that there were no mice out here, but the image of them writhing in her bed was still unbearably vivid in her mind.

She scrambled to her feet and ran into her father's arms.

Above the thundering of her own heart, she could hear noises coming from the open trapdoor. Hard gnawing sounds — the clatter of tiny claws — and deep, hollow, groaning creaks that echoed eerily in the roof.

"What's that?" Katie murmured, staring up at the ceiling.

"Just more of the filthy little beggars," her father

said grimly, his arms wrapped protectively around her. "Well, that does it. This has gotten completely out of control. We're leaving right this minute — until we get the exterminators back in, at least." He put his hands on her shoulders and looked at her. "Go down and find yourself some clean clothes from the laundry room," he told her, his voice reassuringly calm and steady. He stared up at the black hole of the trapdoor. "I'm just going to take a quick look up there. Then we're going to your Aunt Julie's — and you'll be perfectly safe there till we solve this problem."

"But it's the middle of the night," Katie said. "Everyone will be asleep."

"Then we'll just have to wake them up," her father said with an encouraging smile. "They won't mind under the circumstances. Down you go, Katie. Quickly now."

Katie ran down the stairs. She turned on the hallway light, staring anxiously around herself, half convinced that the entire floor would be swarming with the sickening creatures. She couldn't see any mice, but that didn't mean they weren't close by and creeping around — keeping out of sight in the shadows. Katie shivered. Her home had become a horrible, terrifying place to be. The sooner she got out of there, the better.

She made her way gingerly toward the laundry room, watching every footstep, dreading to see more of the repulsive creatures. There would be fresh clothes in there, and there was a pair of sneakers by the front door. She wouldn't need to go back into her bedroom for anything.

She was about to enter the laundry room when she spotted something out of the corner of her eye — something that lay just inside the threshold of the kitchen door. She narrowed her eyes to peer through the shadows and then jumped. It was furry. A mouse!

But no. It was too big to be a mouse — and it was the wrong color. It was golden brown with black flecks, and it was lying perfectly still on the floor.

She stared at it for a second or two before she realized what it was.

"Crystal!" she gasped in relief. It was the back of her pet's head. *She must be just inside the kitchen doorway, waiting for the perfect opportunity to pounce,* Katie thought.

The Trap

"There's too many for you, Crystal," she said, approaching the open kitchen door. "We have to go now. I'll get your carrier in a minute. You're coming with us. We're all going to . . ."

Her voice trailed off. Crystal's tail was perfectly still on the floor. As Katie walked slowly forward, more of the unmoving animal came into view. She realized that her pet was crouching with her back feet stretched out at an awkward angle.

"Crystal . . . what are you doing, girl?" Katie asked uneasily. Now that she was almost at the kitchen doorway, she could see the hips and back end of the cat, and she saw that she was partially draped across a piece of wood.

What wood? There was no wood in the kitchen . . . except . . .

No! Crystal . . . ?

. . . except for that big old display trap that her father had placed against the wall in there.

And Crystal's tail was caught in it! The cat meowed sadly as she struggled to pull herself free.

Katie was vaguely aware of her father's voice, booming echoey and loud from up in the attic. She hardly even registered the words he said. "Good Lord!" came the faint sound of his voice. "How on earth did these get up here?"

But Katie had eyes only for the terrible thing that lay in front of her on the kitchen floor.

"Crystal . . ." she murmured, her whole body trembling as she edged closer. "What have they done to you?"

With much effort, she pried the thick metal spring bar away from Crystal's tail. The cat darted in the direction of the back door, but Katie was too distracted to let Crystal out. She had spotted something that chilled her to the bone.

There were pieces of ham on the trap.

Scraps of the same ham that Katie thought Crystal had taken yesterday evening.

Too shocked and horrified even to scream, Katie ran back to the stairs. She struggled to breathe as she dragged herself up the stairs, the tears flooding down her face, blinding her.

This wasn't real — it couldn't be happening. It was too awful.

Halfway up the stairs, she was brought to a sudden

halt by a loud crash that came rumbling down from above her, making the whole house shudder. It almost took her legs out from under her.

She stared up. Dust was filtering down. There was a strange silence now — except for the sound of the blood rushing through her head.

"Dad?" she called tentatively, slowly dragging one reluctant foot after the other up the remaining stairs to the landing. "Dad? Are you OK?"

More dust was raining down through the illuminated hole of the trapdoor.

She walked falteringly to the bottom of the ladder. "Dad?" Her voice was hardly more than a breath. She coughed as the dust filled her nose and mouth.

Very slowly, she began to climb the ladder, hand over hand, foot after foot, her tears washing the dust out of her eyes.

Her head and shoulders came up through the hole. The dust was much thicker in here, hanging in the air in dense curtains. It was difficult to see more than vague shapes and shadows in the harsh electric light from the bulb that swung slowly back and forth under the high arched ceiling.

Trembling with fear, Katie clambered up into the attic. She stumbled forward through the haze of dust, coughing and retching as she tried to make her way over the uneven floor.

"Dad . . . ?"

As the dust began to settle, she saw what had made the tumultuous noise. One of the heavy new beams had fallen down. She could see it lying at an odd angle across her path. She put her hand on it, feeling the new wood. Her fingers ran over the uneven surface. It had been pocked and scarred by a thousand vicious teeth.

She saw that the end of the beam had been gnawed through.

The mice had done it. They had gnawed right through a beam that was thicker than Katie's thigh — gnawed at it until it had come crashing down.

Her foot struck against something. She peered down.

It was her father's leg. She reeled back. His face covered in dust, he was caught under the beam like a mouse in a trap.

"Katie," he said weakly. "We've . . . got . . . to . . . get . . . out."

One of his arms was outstretched, as if he had been reaching for something on the other side of the beam when it had come crashing down on him.

Katie looked at the thing his clawing, twisted fingers had been stretching out to grasp.

His car keys.

Katie lunged forward to grab at her dad and try to pull him free of the beam and out of the attic — away from whatever it was that had done this to him! But as she clasped his hand and pulled, her fingers lost their grip and she stumbled backward, hitting against the hanging lightbulb. The light rocked back and forth above her, sending shadows prancing and jumping all around her and her dad like demons.

And then suddenly the lightbulb cracked and spat and died, and the shadows leaped up to smother her. The only light now was a thin filter of gray that came up through the trapdoor.

But then Katie realized that scattered among the gloom of the loft were tiny, wicked eyes: beady red eyes that stared malevolently at her from all directions.

Her survival instincts took control of her actions. She had to find help. She crawled toward the gray square of light in the floor.

But as she moved across the rough floorboards, whimpering and moaning in her fear, the trapdoor slammed shut. Katie was plunged into absolute, impenetrable blackness.

She huddled in the corner, her knees tight up to her chest, her arms crooked to cover her head as she curled up on the floor.

And as she lay there, helpless in the stifling darkness, she heard the scrabble of claws all around her.

The teeming hordes of mice closed in.

STICKS AND STONES

If I'm going to do well at the audition and get the leading role in the play," Kelly Thompson said, "I'm going to need all the luck I can get!"

It was Friday afternoon, and Kelly and her best friend, Nicole Marshall, had taken a bus to the local mall on their way home from school.

They were both excited about the spring play that the school drama department was planning, and it was their main topic of conversation as they cruised the upper floor of the mall.

"You won't need luck," Nicole replied. "You're the

best actress in the entire school. Mrs. Doyle would have to be crazy not to pick you to be Faith."

The play was a comedy called *Faith, Hope, and Barney Bubbles*. It was a boy-meets-girl, boy-loses-girl, boy-gets-girl-back-for-a-happy-ending kind of story, with Faith and Barney as the two main characters.

Kelly smiled. "You're forgetting Fiona," she said. "She's really good, too."

Nicole shook her head. "Not as good as you." She eyed Kelly sternly. "You know your problem?"

"No, but I'm sure you're going to tell me."

"Yes, I am," Nicole said. "You're too nice, Kelly. You don't stand up for yourself enough. Fiona Oslow is a bigheaded, pushy know-it-all."

"Some people might call that being assertive and confident," Kelly said with a smile.

"So that means you have to be even more assertive and confident than her," Nicole insisted. "That's the difference between winners and losers."

Kelly laughed. "You mean I should act like an even more bigheaded, pushy know-it-all in order to beat her?"

"Kind of — in a nice way," Nicole said with a wry smile.

Kelly didn't feel as sure about this as Nicole did. She enjoyed being part of the drama class and loved acting, but she knew that Fiona was also very good. Fiona had just as much chance of landing the dream role of Faith as she did.

"Hope is a pretty good part, too," Kelly said, linking arms with Nicole as they started walking again. "She gets plenty of nice lines."

"Hope is just Faith's sidekick," Nicole said. "You don't want to be Fiona's sidekick, do you?"

"Not really," Kelly admitted. "But I'm just not the pushy type, Nicole — you know that." She frowned in thought. "The only way I'm going to beat Fiona is if I ace the audition. And that's where you come in. I want you to coach me with the lines. I have to be absolutely word-perfect."

"I can do that," Nicole said. "Just don't expect any great acting from me. Which part do you want me to read?"

"We'll have to do it both ways," Kelly said. "With

me as Hope and you as Faith — and the other way around, too. Mrs. Doyle could ask me to play either part on Monday, so I have to know them both."

"Smart thinking," Nicole said. "Listen, I have to buy some of my mom's vitamins from the health food store. Why don't I dash over there, and we'll meet up outside the west exit and then head on over to your place to do some rehearsing?"

"Sounds good to me," said Kelly.

Nicole headed off across the mall. Kelly strolled in the opposite direction, making for the west exit. From there, it was only a short bus ride and she would be home.

She paused to look in the window of Tinseltown Rebellion, a popular store that sold fashion accessories. They had some really nice stuff in the window. If Kelly got the part of Faith, she'd consider buying a necklace and a few of their silvery bracelets as props. They weren't especially expensive and they'd look great.

She noticed that the place next door had its windows blacked out. She tried to remember what kind of store it had been, but for some reason she couldn't quite remember. A travel agent's? No, that wasn't right. A clothing store? *How weird*, she thought. *I must have walked past it dozens of times and now I don't have a clue what it was.*

The other weird thing was that its door was wide open. Soft, dreamy music drifted out.

Intrigued, Kelly walked over to the open door and peered inside. There was a light in there, but it was dim and red and she couldn't really make much out.

"Come right in," called a friendly woman's voice. "We're open for business, you know."

Kelly stepped over the threshold and found herself in a fairly normal-looking store. The only peculiar thing was that once inside it was far brighter than it seemed to be from the outside.

It looked like an old-fashioned pharmacy, with shelves full of cough remedies and toothpicks, hairnets, and large colored bottles with glass stoppers. The labels on these bottles were strange. Kelly read one of them: ANTEPHELIC MILK. FOR THE SKIN OF THE FACE. REMOVES FRECKLES, SUNBURN, RED SPOTS, PIMPLES, BLACKHEADS, FEVER BLISTERS, AND WRINKLES.

Huh? Kelly thought, walking slowly along the shelf. She couldn't even pronounce that antephel-whatever word — let alone make sense of what it meant.

The other bottles were just as strange:

YOUTH AND BEAUTY. LILLIE POWDER FOR THE COMPLEXION!

SHINING TRESSES WITH AMAMI SHAMPOO — GUARANTEED PURE BY THE INSTITUTE OF HEALTH!

TOILET VINEGAR.

Wha-at? Kelly stared in disbelief at the handwritten label. *Who buys all this weird stuff?*

"You're very welcome to browse, my dear," said the woman.

"I didn't think you were open," Kelly said, moving between the shelving units and spotting the woman standing behind a counter at the far end of the store. She had been just about to walk out when the woman spoke, but she didn't want to appear rude. Not that there was anything in here that she'd want to buy in a million years!

"We're not always easy to find," the woman said. "But it's worth it for those who persevere."

Kelly gave her a puzzled look. That had been an unusual thing to say. What kind of store expects customers to *persevere?*

But the woman looked perfectly normal. Kelly guessed that she was probably in her fifties, with short gray hair and a round, smiling face behind horn-rimmed glasses. She was wearing a frilly white blouse and a plaid skirt, and she had an accent that sounded like it might be Scottish.

"It's really strange," Kelly said. "I come to the mall all the time, but I don't remember seeing this place before."

The woman came around from behind the counter. "Oh, this is a very old store, my dear," she said. "Very well established, you might say." She looked closely into Kelly's face. "Well, aren't you the prettiest girl in the whole wide world, now?" she said. "With those big blue eyes and with such a lovely head of fine golden hair. I have a special herbal shampoo in stock that would make it shine like the sun."

Kelly blushed under the woman's close scrutiny.

People commenting on her looks always made her

self-conscious. "I have to use special shampoo," she said. "I'm allergic to a lot of stuff. My skin gets all pimply."

"Well, you don't want that, do you?" purred the woman in her soft, warm voice. "Not with those movie-star looks." She smiled. "Do you act at all, my dear?"

Kelly gave her a startled look. "Well, yes," she said. "Only at school . . . but how did you guess that?"

"Ahh, it's a cutthroat business, the acting world," the woman said, as if she hadn't heard the question. "A person can have all the talent in the world, but if they don't have a touch of luck, then it can all be for nothing." Her eyes shone behind her eyeglasses. "Do you know what I mean?"

"Um . . . I guess so . . ." Kelly said. She had said something similar to Nicole only a few minutes ago.

The woman lifted a finger. "It just so happens I have the very thing for an aspiring actress, right here in this store. Arrived today. Just you wait there a moment, my dear."

The woman went back behind the counter and stooped to rummage around underneath. Kelly watched her with amused curiosity.

The woman stood up straight and placed something on the counter.

Kelly walked over to look at it. It was a small, wide glass jar with a twist-off lid.

"There now," the woman said. "How about that?"

Kelly picked up the little jar. There was something thick inside. It was slightly rose-tinted, although that could have been the lights in the store.

SHINY TIME was written on the lid of the jar. And underneath, in smaller letters: LIP GLOSS FOR SPECIAL OCCASIONS.

"Oh — lip gloss," Kelly said. "Sorry — I don't use lip gloss. My mom doesn't approve after I went a little crazy last summer wearing some, um, interesting shades. Anyway, it's not allowed at school."

"Your mom couldn't object to this," the woman said. "It's virtually transparent. And I have it on sale today. You could easily afford it and still have plenty of money left over."

Kelly hesitated. It was a cute little jar, and she did like the idea of the transparent lip gloss. After all . . . was that really makeup? It would only make her lips bright and shiny.

"Oh, why not? I'll take it!" she said with a smile.

She paid up and the woman put the jar into a little red bag before handing it back over the counter.

"You won't believe the effect it has on the people around you when you put just a little dab of it on your lips," the woman called as Kelly headed for the door. "You simply won't believe it!"

Kelly met up with Nicole a few minutes later, and the two of them hopped on a bus to Kelly's house. On the way, Kelly told Nicole about the weird store and showed her the jar of lip gloss.

"That's strange, I don't remember that place, either," Nicole said, unscrewing the little jar and sniffing at the contents. "Mmm . . . nice." She looked at Kelly. "The woman was totally loony, huh?"

"No, not really," Kelly said. "Not loony — just a little . . . *unusual*. She guessed right away that I like acting." Kelly gave a quick, bashful smile. "She said I looked like a movie star."

"Well, you do," Nicole said. "And when you're rich and famous, I want to come and stay at your million-aire mansion."

"It's a deal," Kelly said with a laugh. "You'll be my very first houseguest."

They arrived at Kelly's house to find her mom out in the driveway, washing the family car in the bright afternoon sunshine. Kelly had put the little glass jar into her book bag. She had decided that it would be wise for her to be cautious about how and when to introduce the idea of lip gloss to her mom.

"Hello, girls," Mrs. Thompson said, straightening up after wiping the front bumper. "How was your day?"

"It was OK," Kelly said.

"There's juice and some salads in the fridge if you want to eat now," her mother said. "Or you can wait and I'll cook something a little later."

"Later is good," Kelly said. "We've got some rehearsing to do."

"Don't you have an audition coming up?" her mom asked.

"Yes — and Nicole's going to help me learn the lines."

"Would you please check in on Stacey first?" her

mom said. "She's got Paula over, and you know what those two are like when they get together."

"Will do," Kelly said as she and Nicole headed into the house. "Why don't you get some cans of Coke from the fridge while I check on my little sister?"

Nicole disappeared into the kitchen, and Kelly climbed the stairs. Halfway up, she called out, "Mom says to stop that right this minute!"

There was the sound of furtive voices from above and the noise of scampering feet across the landing.

Kelly leaped up the rest of the stairs in time to see her seven-year-old sister, Stacey, and her pal Paula bolting into Stacey's bedroom. The door to their parents' bedroom was open.

"Have you gotten into Mom's stuff again?" Kelly called.

"No!" came the shrill response.

"Yeah — right!" said Kelly. "I so believe that!" She strode across the landing and shoved Stacey's bedroom door open.

Stacey's face was covered in badly applied makeup — deep red lipstick, blue eyeliner, and circles of rouge that had been smeared unevenly on her cheeks. Paula looked almost as bad.

Stacey glared defiantly at her big sister. "Get out of my room, Kelly!" she said.

"What *do* you two think you look like?" Kelly said with a splutter of laughter. "You know how Mom feels about you messing with her makeup bag."

"Mind your own business!" Stacey retorted. "If you tell on us, I'll hate you forever, freak face!" Paula, meanwhile, looked down at her feet, saying nothing.

"Yeah, yeah, yeah!" Kelly taunted. "But remember what Grandma always tells us," she said, and then she recited their grandma's old saying in a singsong voice that she knew would drive her little sister wild. "Sticks and stones may break my bones — but names will never hurt me."

"Kelly, you are such a *loser!*" Stacey said, shaking her head.

Kelly shrugged her shoulders, feigning indifference. "What*ever!*" she said. "Anyway, Mom knew you were up to no good. You were being too quiet."

Nicole arrived at the bedroom door with the cans of soda. She peered at Stacey and Paula over Kelly's shoulder. "Oh, look — the circus is in town!" she said, bursting out laughing.

Stacey stuck her tongue out at her.

"Charming," Nicole said. "One day, you'll get stuck looking like that."

"If I did, I'd still be better-looking than you," Stacey retorted.

Nicole grinned. "Whatever, Stacey," she said.

"Bye-bye, Stacey, be a good little girl, now," Kelly said, backing out of her sister's room and shutting the door.

They went along the hall to Kelly's room. Kelly dumped her book bag on the bed and rummaged through it for her copy of the scene that she had to learn for the audition.

The jar of lip gloss rolled out.

"Hey — try it out," Nicole suggested. "I want to see how you look in it."

Kelly unscrewed the jar and dipped a finger inside. Leaning over her dressing-table mirror, she wiped the glistening goo across her lips.

"Wow!" she said, looking at her reflection. "Shiny or

what?" She turned and smiled at Nicole. "Does it show at all?"

"Arrgh!" Nicole cringed back, covering her eyes with her hands, pretending to be blinded. "Does it *show?*" she said. "That's got to be the glossiest lip gloss I've ever seen!"

Kelly turned to her reflection again. "It *is* kind of bright, isn't it?" she said. She tried a big wide smile. "I like it, though."

"So do I," Nicole agreed. "So? Are we going to rehearse, or what?"

"We're going to rehearse," Kelly said.

And for the next hour or so, the two friends went through the audition scene until Kelly knew both parts backward.

She was determined to do her best at the auditions. She could hardly wait.

On Saturday morning, Kelly decided to give her new lip gloss a trial run at home. Before she went down to breakfast, she unscrewed the jar. She sniffed the clear pinkish gel. It smelled nice — like roses. She scooped up a little on her fingertip and smoothed it over her lips.

She looked at the result in the mirror. Her lips were bright and shiny again.

"I love it!" she said to her reflection. "I love it to pieces!"

She headed downstairs.

The aroma of fresh toast filled the kitchen. Dad was at the table, reading a golfing magazine. Mom was at the countertop, smearing a layer of chocolate hazelnut spread onto a couple of slices of toast. Kelly assumed that Stacey was still asleep in bed.

"Hi," Kelly said, taking a pitcher of orange juice from the fridge and pouring herself a glass.

"Hello, sweetheart," her dad murmured without looking up.

"Hello, there," her mom said, smoothing the thick chocolate spread out into all corners of the toast.

"What a nice day," Kelly said, looking out of the window.

"Perfect weather for golf this afternoon!" said her father, still not looking up.

"And for some gardening, for those of us who have a lawn to mow and flowers to water," her mother said pointedly.

Kelly frowned at them. Why wouldn't they look at her? She wanted to find out how they'd react to the lip gloss. She felt pretty sure that her mom couldn't take offense to this one.

"Uh, Mom, Dad," she said hesitantly. "What do you think of my lip gloss?"

Her father looked up at her. "It's very shiny," he said. "Make sure you don't blind anybody with it."

Typical Dad! Kelly thought.

She looked anxiously at her mom.

"It suits you," she said, eyeing Kelly closely. "It's a lot better than that stuff you were wearing last summer! But if you're planning on wearing it to school, you'd better put it on a little less thickly, or they'll make you wipe it all off!"

Kelly let out a relieved breath. "I thought you'd hate it," she said.

"It's only lip gloss," her mom said. "I don't object to lip gloss. But let's keep it at that for the time being, OK? No other makeup just yet. Got it?"

"Got it!" Kelly said as she sat down at the table. "Could you fix me some of what you're having, please?"

"Sorry," her mom replied, bringing the plate and sitting opposite her. "That was the last of the chocolate spread. There's peanut butter and jelly and other stuff, though. Help yourself."

"If you were a really kind and considerate mom," Kelly said, half jokingly, "you'd give one of those sweet and delicious slices of toast to me."

Her mom looked at her. "And why on earth would I do that?" she said with a laugh.

"Because you love me more than life itself," Kelly said, reaching across the table. "Please? Give one to me!" she said playfully.

Her mom snatched the plate away. "No way!" she said. "They're mine!" She took a huge bite out of a slice of toast and sat back, grinning.

"Well, I hope you enjoy it!" said Kelly playfully. "Just don't bite off more than you can chew."

A moment later, Kelly's mom let out an anguished and muffled yell. She dropped the plate onto the table and got up, her hand to her mouth.

"What's wrong?" Mr. Thompson asked, jolted away from his magazine. "What have you done?"

"I've bitten my tongue!" wailed Kelly's mom. "Ow! That is so painful!" Grimacing, she shoved the plate across the table toward Kelly. "There! You can have the rest! That hurts!" She stood up. "I'm going to the bathroom to rinse out with some mouthwash."

Kelly looked at her. "I'm sorry," she said. "I didn't mean for that to happen."

Her mom smiled at her as she headed for the door. "It wasn't your fault."

"Poor Mom," Kelly said as her mother left the kitchen.

"I'm sure she'll be fine," her father said. "It was good luck for you, though," he added. "Now you get to eat both slices of toast."

Kelly's new lip gloss had passed the first test: Her mom had not objected. Kelly was really pleased about that. Somehow, wearing the lip gloss made her feel much more self-assured and confident. She didn't know why, exactly — it just did. As she sparingly applied the lip gloss first thing on Monday morning, she wondered how well it would go over at school. Her best hope was that Mrs. Goose, her homeroom teacher, wouldn't even notice it.

But by first period, it looked like her hope would be short-lived — thanks entirely to Fiona Oslow.

"Mrs. Goose!" Fiona called. Kelly looked up from her desk, sensing that Fiona was up to something. She had that all-too-innocent look on her face that always meant trouble and she was waving her arm in the air. It was annoying that someone as sneaky and irritating as Fiona had such a sweet, innocent face, framed with curly red hair and topped off by those big baby-blue eyes of hers.

"What do you want, Fiona?" Mrs. Goose asked.

"Mrs. Goose, what are the rules about wearing makeup to school?" Fiona sang out.

Kelly shot daggers from her eyes — right at Fiona. She'd encountered Fiona briefly on the way to school. Fiona had obviously noticed the lip gloss and was intent on drawing their homeroom teacher's attention to it — presumably with the hope of getting Kelly into trouble.

"You know perfectly well," Mrs. Goose replied. "No girl is allowed to wear any makeup in school. Also forbidden are earrings, any rings or bracelets, and also visible necklaces, pins, and nail polish."

"Does that mean *absolutely* no makeup?" Fiona persisted. "What about lip gloss? Are we allowed to wear lip gloss?"

That's it! thought Kelly. *She's done it now. Here we go!*

Mrs. Goose sighed and gave Fiona a sharp look. "In your case, Fiona, lip *glue* would be a much better idea. I'd have no objection to that at all. Now pipe down, please, so I can take attendance."

"You know what that was all about, don't you?" Nicole murmured in Kelly's ear. "Don't give her the satisfaction of knowing she's annoyed you. Remember the auditions."

Kelly nodded and gave Fiona a big, wide smile.

Fiona glared back.

Kelly was on her way to class when Fiona made her next move. She suddenly stepped out from behind a row of lockers into Kelly's path.

Startled, Kelly stopped in her tracks.

"Makeup won't help, you know," Fiona said evenly. Kelly could see the challenge in Fiona's eyes. Daring Kelly to stand up to her.

"Help what?" Kelly said uncertainly, playing for time. She had no idea what she'd done to rattle Fiona's cage so much. A little healthy competition in auditions — what was the problem there?

"Help you get the part!" Fiona said, her voice a touch louder. "The lead part's mine!" Fiona brought her face an inch or so closer to Kelly's. "And just you remember that!"

Kelly managed a thin smile. "The lead part goes to whoever is the best actor. And I wish you all the luck in the world." Fiona was being a bully, and the best way to handle bullies? Smother them in niceness.

Fiona's eyes narrowed. "Hope you get what you deserve, too," she said, before turning on her heel. Kelly watched her stride down the hallway and let a sigh of relief escape her.

Kelly managed to avoid any contact with Fiona throughout the rest of the school day. She walked over to Mrs. Doyle's classroom after her final class ended. Now the only thing she had to worry about was giving the best audition she possibly could.

Kelly glanced around the room, noticing with surprise that Fiona wasn't there yet. *Wouldn't it be really great if she didn't turn up in time for the auditions?* Kelly said to herself. *That would be just* perfect.

But Kelly's hopes were dashed when the door opened and Mrs. Doyle came in — accompanied by Fiona. Kelly's spirits sank even lower as Fiona walked into the room. She'd completely transformed herself. She wore a short, red crushed-velvet dress, her hair was up, and she'd applied some discreet makeup so that she looked about five years older than she really was.

Kelly's heart sank to her knees. Why hadn't she thought of doing that? She reached into her bag and hastily smoothed some lip gloss over her lips. It was better than nothing.

Fiona glided elegantly across the room and sat with her hands folded in her lap, a sweet little smile on her face. She didn't even look at Kelly.

"OK," said Mrs. Doyle. "First of all, thank you all for coming. As you know there are only three major roles in the play. However, there are another ten speaking parts, so every one of you should get to do something." She leaned against her desk and consulted some notes attached to a clipboard. "Now, hopefully you all know the pieces that I chose for the auditions — so what we're going to do is to go into the auditorium in pairs, where I'll see you perform." She glanced at the clipboard. "I'll do the Faith and Hope auditions first. So just be patient, you boys, and I'll get to you in a little while," she said. "All right, the first pair will be Kim and Megan. And then I'll see Kelly and . . . um . . . Fiona."

Rats, rats, and more rats! thought Kelly. She had been hoping to perform opposite Kim; Fiona was the last person she felt like auditioning with — especially now that Fiona looked so good.

Mrs. Doyle led the two girls out of the room. Kelly sighed, trying to forget Fiona and concentrate on the first lines of the piece. She just had to remember them — and then the rest would come naturally. She knew she had both parts down cold.

Someone sat down beside her. It was Fiona.

"I told you a little lip gloss wasn't going to help you

upstage me," Fiona whispered, looking annoyingly sophisticated, and still smiling that knife-sharp smile of hers. "I'm going to blow you off the stage!"

Kelly swallowed an angry response. She didn't have Fiona's talent for fake smiles, but she did her very best. "Look, Fiona," she said calmly. "I know we don't get along, but I really would like to wish you the best of luck with the audition."

Fiona's eyes narrowed with contempt. "You idiot!" she hissed. "Don't you know anything? You don't wish people good luck on stage — you say 'break a leg,' dimwit."

Kelly could have kicked herself because she *did* know that. She'd been talking about it with her mom and Nicole only the other day!

She managed to keep her cool. "Fair enough, then," she said, still smiling. "Fiona — I really hope you break a leg . . . *dimwit!*" And with that she got up and walked off to the other end of the room.

S̲o what happened?" Nicole asked as Kelly came walking out of the school gates half an hour later.

"Fiona wiped the floor with me," Kelly mumbled.

Nicole frowned. "What? Never! How?"

Kelly sighed. "She dressed up for the part," she said. "She put on makeup. She looked great. And I just looked like a school kid!" She gave a heavy sigh. "Mrs. Doyle was thrilled with Fiona for doing so much preparation." She mimicked the drama teacher's voice. "*Oh, Fiona, that's just perfect for Faith. Oh, Fiona, that's such marvelous characterization.*"

"You didn't forget your lines, though, did you?" Nicole asked anxiously. "It wasn't as bad as that?"

Kelly tapped her head. "Oh, yes it was. Of course, I can remember them all now," she said. "I could do the scene backward, now! But it's too late. Fiona gets to be Faith — and I get to be her idiot pal Hope."

Nicole tried to look optimistic. "It could have been worse," she said.

"Could it? How? From now on, I get to play a wall-flower alongside Fiona."

"Listen," said Nicole. "Let's go to the mall and I'll buy you an ice cream. That always cheers you up. What do you say?"

Kelly gave her friend a weak smile. "Why not? It certainly couldn't make me feel any worse than I do right now."

They headed for the bus stop.

Well, Kelly thought gloomily, *so much for the confidence-building power of Shiny Time lip gloss.* What had that woman in the store told her? *"You won't believe the effect it has on the people around you when you put just a little dab of it on your lips."*

Well, now she knew the effect — absolutely nothing!

The ice cream did help a little. Kelly knew she wouldn't be down in the dumps for long. It just wasn't her style. And Nicole was always great at cheering her up. By the time Kelly had finished her ice cream, she was feeling much more positive about life. After all — she was in the play. If she worked hard and pulled out all the stops, there was no reason why she couldn't act Fiona right off the stage.

"And now you can show me that store where you bought the lip gloss," Nicole said. "I've just got to meet that weird woman you told me about."

Kelly smiled. "She wasn't *weird*, exactly," she said as the two friends made their way along the upper level of the mall. "She was just a little . . . eccentric."

"Eccentric is polite for weird," Nicole said.

Kelly laughed. "Maybe."

Her laughter died as they turned the corner and came to the place where the store had been. The window was boarded up, and there was a padlock on the door.

"Looks like they've gone belly-up or something," Nicole said, stepping up to the door and rattling the padlock. She peered in through the glass door panel. "There's nothing in there — not a thing." She looked around at Kelly. "So much for that idea."

Kelly frowned. What could have happened to make the store shut down within a few days of her being in there?

"I'm going to find out if these people know anything about it," she said, pointing toward Tinseltown Rebellion, the accessories store. The two of them went into the store, pushing their way through the tight-packed racks of necklaces, scarves, earrings, hats, and belts.

A young woman was busy stacking shoes.

"Excuse me," Kelly said. "That place next door — do you know when they closed?"

The young woman looked at her. "About two months ago," she said.

Kelly stared at her. "Excuse me?"

The young woman nodded. "It was a stationery store," she said. "They sold off their inventory and packed up."

"No." Kelly shook her head. "I was in there last Friday. It was sort of like a cosmetics store."

The woman gave her a puzzled look. "I don't think so," she said. "As far as I know, there hasn't been anyone at all in there recently — certainly not a place like that."

"That's ridiculous," Kelly said. "I bought some lip gloss. The store was full of stuff. And there was a Scottish lady there, in her fifties or sixties, with gray hair."

The woman shook her head slowly. "Sorry," she said. "I can't help you there. Maybe someone was checking out the place?"

"But it was full of items for sale," Kelly insisted. "You must have noticed it."

The assistant blinked at her. "Sorry."

A customer called for help and the store clerk wandered off.

Kelly and Nicole looked at each other.

"You're sure it was *here*?" Nicole asked. "Maybe it was somewhere else and you just got confused?"

Kelly marched out of the store and stood staring at the boarded-up storefront next door. "No, I didn't get confused," she said. "It was there."

Nicole shrugged. "Either way, it's gone now," she said. "Do you want to come back to my place for a while? Mom's making tacos."

Nicole's mother made excellent tacos, so Kelly didn't have to think too long about that.

They headed toward the exit.

"Oh, great," Nicole groaned. "That's all we need!"

Kelly turned in the direction Nicole was looking. Fiona and her nasty sidekick Tanya Barker were sitting on the top step of the stairs, eating pizza. There was no way to avoid them without making it obvious.

"Let's go another way," Nicole urged.

"No way!" Kelly said. "I'm not scared of them."

"Neither am I," Nicole muttered. "I'd just prefer to avoid a fistfight, that's all."

"Chill out, Nicole," Kelly said softly. "Nothing's going to happen."

Kelly walked toward the stairs, her head held high, totally ignoring the two girls. She intended to step between them without even acknowledging their existence.

But Fiona obviously didn't plan on being ignored.

She stood up and blocked Kelly's path.

"Still hanging around with nerds?" she asked, casting a spiteful glance in Nicole's direction.

Kelly looked at her. "Still using that dumb brain?" she replied, secretly delighted to have thought of an instant comeback.

Fiona glowered at her. "You can't act to save your life — it's pathetic!" she mocked. "I'm going to go to Mrs. Doyle first thing tomorrow and tell her that I want Kim to play Hope. At least she's not a total loser."

Tanya snorted with laughter from her seat at the head of the stairs. "Total loser!" she echoed.

"Oh, get out of my way," Kelly said. "And take your pet monkey with you!"

Kelly moved forward, intending to shoulder her

way past Fiona. But before they made any contact, Fiona took a sidestep. What happened next was so sudden and so awful that Kelly could hardly believe her eyes.

Fiona bumped into Tanya and stumbled backward, her face filled with panic and her arms windmilling as she teetered on the very brink of the stairs.

"He-elp!" Fiona yelled in a panicked shriek.

Kelly made a grab for her, but before she could even grab hold of her clothes, Fiona went tumbling down the stairs like a rag doll.

Kelly stared in horror as Fiona fell. The whole world seemed to have slipped into hideous slow motion. It took forever before Fiona finally crashed onto the floor at the bottom of the stairs.

There was a moment's silence. Then people began to run toward her from all over, calling out for help.

Tanya just sat on the top step with her mouth hanging open and her eyes bulging. Kelly raced down the stairs.

Fiona sat up, propping herself on her arms. She looked dazed and bewildered and in obvious pain.

Kelly winced as she saw the weird way that Fiona's

right leg was lying: twisted out sideways at a freaky angle.

"Don't touch her!" someone shouted. "Call an ambulance. She's broken her leg!"

The next morning, Kelly was still having awful flashbacks of the terrible accident. As she sat on the school wall in between classes, another vivid memory was interrupted when a younger student shook her shoulder and told her that Mrs. Doyle wanted to see her.

"Ah, Kelly," Mrs. Doyle said when Kelly appeared at the teacher's classroom door. "Have you heard about what happened to Fiona? She fell down the stairs at the mall yesterday afternoon. She's broken her leg in two places."

"I know," Kelly said with a gulp. "I was there."

"Were you? Oh, dear — I imagine that must have been quite a shock."

"It was," Kelly agreed. "Her leg was all twisted around." She shuddered. "It was horrible."

Mrs. Doyle nodded. "The thing is, Kelly, there's no way that Fiona is going to be able to star in the play now."

"Oh!" Kelly hadn't even thought about that. "Are you canceling it?"

"I hardly think we need to do that," said Mrs. Doyle. "In Fiona's unfortunate absence, I'd like you to take on the role of Faith. I'm going to have a word with Kim Forrest and ask her if she'd like to play Hope. I think the two of you will work well together." She looked at Kelly. "Are you OK with that?"

Kelly gazed at her, hardly able to believe her luck. "Yes! Yes, of course," she said.

"I know you wouldn't have wanted to get this part in such a terrible way," Mrs. Doyle continued. "But I also know you'll do a first-class job. All right — you can go now. And when you see Kim, could you tell her to come and see me, please?"

"Yes," Kelly muttered. "Of course." She walked out of the classroom in a daze.

She went to her next class, slipping into her seat beside Nicole.

"What did Mrs. Doyle want?" Nicole hissed.

"Fiona's out of the play," Kelly said breathlessly. "And I'm playing Faith!"

"It's that lip gloss!" Nicole hissed. "If we hadn't gone looking for the store where you bought the lip gloss, we wouldn't have met up with Fiona like that yesterday afternoon. She wouldn't have been trying to get at you — and she wouldn't have tripped over that bratty pal of hers!" Nicole grinned widely at Kelly. "It's got to be lucky lip gloss!"

Kelly nodded. Maybe Nicole was right. Maybe the lip gloss was bringing her good luck after all . . . but it had only done that at the expense of some very bad luck for Fiona Oslow.

Not that Kelly was going to lose much sleep over *that*!

Kelly's good mood didn't last for the entire morning. She was in a stall in the girls' room when she heard Fiona's pal Tanya talking to some other girls in there.

"Of course, you know that Kelly Fish-lips pushed Fiona down the stairs on purpose, don't you?"

"No-o-o!" came the voices of her small audience.

"It's totally true," Tanya continued. "I was there — I saw the whole thing. And if Fish-lips thinks she can get away with that, she's got another thing coming.

There's going to be some serious payback coming to that girl, I can promise you that!"

Kelly didn't want a confrontation with Tanya, so she kept out of sight until the girls were all gone. She wasn't scared of Tanya, but she was an awful piece of work. She was a bully, but like all bullies, she couldn't deal with anyone who stood up to her. Pushing around other kids was Tanya's favorite pastime — and Kelly was not about to let herself be pushed around.

School had just finished for the day. Nicole was off playing basketball, but Kelly was trying out for the field hockey team, and this afternoon there was going to be a play-off to pick people for a big interschool competition.

Before getting changed in the locker room, Kelly quickly freshened her lip gloss. It wouldn't do any harm to give herself a boost out on the athletic field this afternoon.

She was lacing her sneakers when Tanya loomed over her. Her heavy hockey stick rested against her shoulder.

Kelly took a deep breath and stood up. "Do you want something?" she asked.

"Me?" Tanya said. "No, I don't want anything. I just thought I ought to warn you to be really careful out there today." She poked Kelly in the chest with the butt end of the stick. "You might get hurt."

"Oh, go away," Kelly said impatiently. "You're totally useless without Fiona to back you up. You don't scare me, Tanya. Your brain is so feeble that you don't even know where you are half the time. You're a total deadhead!" Kelly pushed past Tanya and headed for the way out.

She didn't feel quite as confident as she hoped she had sounded. Tanya's comments had been a definite threat. Suddenly, the field hockey game didn't seem like it was going to be quite as much fun as Kelly had anticipated — not if Tanya was looking for a chance to take her down with that stick of hers!

Within a minute of the game starting, Kelly got the ball. She gave a well-practiced flick of her stick, and the ball went skimming between her opponent's legs, right onto the stick of one of her own team.

There was an open goal. "Whack it!" Kelly yelled.

Her teammate swung the stick and the ball went flying. But she hit it from an awkward angle and the ball zoomed through the air in entirely the wrong direction.

The ball cracked off the back of Tanya's head, and she went down like a felled tree.

The referee blew the whistle as Kelly and everyone else crowded around Tanya, who lay stretched out on the ground facedown. The coach crouched beside her and gently turned Tanya onto her back. She blinked dizzily up at them.

"Where am I?" she murmured. "What happened? What's going on?"

"You were hit by the ball," the coach said. "Let's get you inside."

Tanya was helped to her feet, and the coach picked two people to accompany her off the field.

Kelly did her best to suppress a grin as Tanya walked back to the changing rooms.

So much for Tanya Barker's plans for revenge, Kelly thought. And wasn't it funny how her two greatest enemies had been erased from the picture within a couple of days?

She licked her lips, tasting the lucky gloss.

The playground was full of gossip about Tanya the next morning.

Kim came running up to Kelly and Nicole as they arrived at school. "Tanya was taken to the emergency room at the hospital," she told them. "They kept her overnight for observation."

"What did they observe?" Kelly asked.

"Well, I just heard from Jordan that the doctors didn't find anything wrong with her apart from a mild concussion." Jordan was another of Tanya's pals.

"Huh!" said Nicole. "They couldn't have been looking very hard. I can tell you plenty of things that are wrong with Tanya."

Kelly wasn't sure how she felt. Tanya wasn't getting very much sympathy.

"Jordan said that Tanya's mom is keeping her out of school for a few days," Kim told them. "Apparently she called Jordan's mom and said that she was worried

about Tanya because she's such a sensitive child." All
three of them howled with laughter at that.

"She's about as sensitive as a rock," Kelly said. "I'm
sorry that Tanya got hurt and I would never have
wished it on her — but it does kind of serve her right
for telling people I pushed Fiona down the stairs in
the mall."

Nicole grinned at her. "That's both Tanya and Fiona
out of your hair for a while," she said. "That lip gloss is
amazing!"

Kim gave them a puzzled look. "What are you talking about?"

"Nicole's got this theory that my new lip gloss is
giving me lots of good luck," Kelly said.

Kim's eyes widened. "You're kidding! Really?"

Kelly laughed. "No, of course not really!" she said.
"We're just joking." She rolled her eyes. "Lucky lip
gloss!" she said. "As if!"

It was a week later. Kelly emerged from the school
auditorium at the end of the school day after a long
rehearsal session for the play. She took a deep breath
of fresh air, glad to be outside for a change.

She reached into her bag and took out the jar of lip gloss, smoothing the gloss over her lips. As the date for the performance loomed, everyone in the drama group was rehearsing as much as they could. Leisurely lunch breaks were a thing of the past.

Today they had rehearsed the final scene — where Faith and Barney finally get together. It involved them kissing.

Kelly had been nervous about having to kiss David, who played Barney, right there onstage. And of course, she had frozen mid-scene as his face came looming toward her.

"Sorry! I can't. I really can't," she spluttered as she instinctively drew away.

Mrs. Doyle had taken her to a quiet room to talk her through the problem.

"Listen," she'd said. "Stage kissing is easy. All you do is put your hands on his face like this." She had rested her two hands on Kelly's cheeks, placing her thumbs across Kelly's mouth. "And then you turn away from the audience as you move in, and you kiss your own thumbs. See? You don't even have to make contact with him."

Kelly felt much better after that. In fact, she had immediately returned to the stage to perform the scene again — and she'd kissed David right on the mouth without being the least bit worried about it.

She smiled as she exited the school building. She was pleased with herself for having overcome her embarrassment. Performing in the play was hard work — but she was certain that the finished product would be worth all the effort!

"Where the heck have you been?" Kelly was snapped out of her happy thoughts by Nicole's voice. Her friend was standing on the front steps of the school looking annoyed.

Kelly stared at her in surprise. "Oh, hello, there. What's wrong with you?" she asked.

"What's wrong with me is that I've been standing here for the last hour waiting for you!" Nicole said irritably. "We were supposed to go to the movies — remember?"

"That's tomorrow," Kelly said.

"No!" Nicole growled. "It's today!"

"Is it really? Are you sure?"

"Yes, I am sure."

"Oh, sorry about that," Kelly said. "I've been at rehearsal — I just forgot." She smiled. "Listen, I had to do the scene where I kiss Barney, and —"

"Kelly, please!" Nicole interrupted her. "You never talk about anything other than that play anymore. You promised to come see the movie — and then you totally forgot about me."

"I'm sorry," Kelly said, surprised by the hurt in her friend's voice. "I didn't mean to upset you. But the play is really important to me right now — you know that."

"Yes," Nicole said. "More important than me, that's really obvious. Some best friend you are!"

"Oh, just shut up and stop being so silly!" Kelly snapped.

Nicole stared angrily at her for a moment. Then she turned on her heel and walked away.

Kelly instantly regretted her outburst. "Nicole?" she called. "I didn't mean it."

But her friend stormed off without saying another word.

Kelly was still feeling bad about her argument with Nicole later that evening. She was supposed to be working on an especially tricky piece of dialogue, but she couldn't concentrate on it. She kept thinking of Nicole.

Finally, she grabbed her cell phone and sent a peace-making text message:

Sorry. Sorry. Sorry. I didn't mean 2 snap at u. Friends? K.

She sat on her bed with the cell phone in her lap, waiting for a response.

None came.

It seemed that Nicole wasn't interested in making up yet.

Fine, Kelly thought, throwing aside the phone. *If she wants to sulk, then let her!* She picked up her script and started reading again.

Only a total moron would prefer apple-walnut muffins to blueberry muffins!" Stacey declared the following morning, giving Kelly a disdainful look across the breakfast table.

"You are out of your tiny mind," Kelly retorted as her sister bit deep into a muffin. "Those blueberries look just like rabbit droppings! In fact, I bet that's exactly what they are!"

Stacey spluttered, spitting out pieces of the muffin. "Do you want to know what an apple-walnut muffin reminds me of?" she said with an evil grin.

"No, I don't!" Kelly said quickly.

"Girls!" said their mother. "I think that's enough about muffins for today."

A moment later, the phone rang and their mother went off to the living room to answer it.

"That was Nicole's mom," she said, coming back into the kitchen. "Nicole's come down with some kind of nasty throat infection, so there's no point in going over there to pick her up on the way to school."

"Poor thing," Kelly said, feeling a stab of guilt. She had assumed that Nicole wasn't responding to her text message because she was having a temper tantrum. "Is it bad?"

"Bad enough for her mom to take her to the doctor's this morning," Kelly's mom said. She looked carefully at Kelly. "Are you feeling OK?"

"Yes — I'm fine."

"Good. Let's hope it stays that way."

"I'm fine, too," Stacey said.

"Well, that's good news as well," said her mom, patting her head.

"I'll go and see her after school," Kelly resolved, determined to make up with Nicole as quickly as possible, especially if she was feeling rotten.

"Not if she's infectious," her mom warned her. "Mrs. Marshall said Nicole has totally lost her voice. You don't want to catch something like that with your play coming up at the end of next week, do you?"

"Definitely not!" Kelly said. She put her hand to her throat. "I hope she hasn't given me anything. That would be a total disaster!"

"I don't think it would be a disaster if you lost your voice," Stacey said with a wide smile. "I think it would be a big improvement!"

Kelly tried texting Nicole a couple of times during the school day, but she didn't get a reply. She stopped off at the Marshalls' house on her way home that evening. Mrs. Marshall answered the door.

"The doctor says it's tonsillitis," said Mrs. Marshall, sighing. "She's completely lost her voice! But she said to give this to you."

It was a small note card with cartoon penguins on it taken from a gift set that Kelly had bought Nicole for her last birthday. Kelly opened it.

Sorry we argued. Mom won't let me use the phone because she says I need to rest and not spend all day texting you! Moms!!! I'll speak to you soon — as soon as I CAN speak! N.

It was two days before Nicole was healthy enough for Kelly to drop in on her again.

She was sitting up in bed, propped up by pillows and surrounded by her collection of stuffed penguin toys. She was even wearing pajamas with cartoon penguins all over them. Nicole had a thing about penguins.

As Kelly walked into her friend's bedroom, Nicole scribbled something with a marker pen on a notepad.

Hi, there!

She smiled and beckoned for Kelly to come and sit on the bed.

"Can't you speak at all?"

Nicole scribbled.

No. Doc says not to try cuz it will hurt throat. How are you?

"I'm absolutely fine," Kelly said. "Listen — that fight we had . . ."

Forget it!

Kelly smiled.

Nicole scribbled for a while again then turned the notepad toward Kelly.

That lucky lip gloss of yours isn't so lucky for people around you, is it?

Kelly gave her a puzzled look. "What do you mean?"

Kelly shuffled up to the top of the bed and sat with

her back to the headboard, so that she could see what her friend was writing as she went along.

You told Fiona to break her leg and she did!!!!

"Well, yes," Kelly admitted. "But that was just a coincidence."

You told me you called Tanya a deadhead and then a few minutes afterward she got hit on the head with a hockey ball and got a concussion!!!!!!!

"OK, that's true," Kelly agreed.
The next thing was written in capital letters and underlined.

<u>YOU TOLD ME TO SHUT UP, AND I LOST MY
VOICE!!!!!!!!!!</u>

Kelly stared at the writing and then at Nicole, who was giving her a very strange look. Nicole wrote something else and banged the end of her pen against the notepad for emphasis.

That's three times it's happened. I'm telling you — something weird is going on.

Kelly laughed. "Are you trying to tell me that you think the lip gloss is responsible for all those things?" she said. She put her hand to Nicole's forehead. "Maybe I should check if you have a fever," she said. "I think your brain's overheating!"

Kelly was sitting at her desk up in her room later that evening. The play script was open in front of her — but she wasn't looking at it. She had her chin in her hands and her elbows on the desk, and for the last ten minutes she had been staring at the small jar of lip gloss that was perched on top of her computer.

Wish-granting lip gloss, she murmured to herself. *As if!*
She picked up the jar and unscrewed the top.

SHINY TIME
LIP GLOSS FOR SPECIAL OCCASIONS

There was no other information on the jar.

She dipped a fingertip and glossed her lips. The whole idea of magic lip gloss was completely ludicrous. She knew exactly how to prove to herself that this was perfectly ordinary, normal, everyday stuff.

She sat back. "I wish . . ." She paused. She had been planning on something huge — like wishing for a million dollars. But she decided to start small.

"I wish Mom would come up here right now with some chocolate ice cream."

She turned to look at the closed bedroom door. She listened for the sound of footsteps on the stairs. There were none.

Of course not! she thought.

"This is just plain silly," she muttered under her breath. "Nothing is going to happen."

She nearly jumped out of her skin as her bedroom door flew open.

"I'm bored," came an all-too-familiar shrill voice. "Want to play something?" Stacey was standing in the doorway.

"I wish you'd learn to open doors like a civilized person!" Kelly shouted at her sister. "I'm busy. Go away. I'll play with you in a little while, OK?"

Stacey's eagle eyes spotted the jar of lip gloss. "Can I try some of that?" she asked, coming into the room.

"No, you can't," Kelly said. "Now go away like a good girl, and I'll come and play with you in a few minutes. As soon as I've finished learning these lines."

"Dumb play," Stacey muttered as she walked out again. "What did I ever do to deserve such a loser for a sister?" The door slammed.

Kelly let out a long breath.

"You see," she said to the jar as she screwed the lid back on. "You're not lucky-wish lip gloss at all. I ask for Mom and chocolate ice cream, and I get Stacey and a lot of attitude!" She paused as an odd memory suddenly popped into her head.

She remembered that Saturday morning when she had gone downstairs wearing the lip gloss for the first time to try it out on her parents. Her mom had made herself some toast with chocolate hazelnut spread on it — and Kelly had asked her to give it to her. *And the very next second, her mom had bitten her tongue and Kelly had gotten the toast after all.*

Kelly's eyes widened.

That made *four* bad things that had happened to people just after she had spoken.

Crazy, she muttered to herself, turning the jar slowly between her fingers. *It's just plain ridiculous!*

There was no real information on the jar — nothing to say where it had been made or what ingredients it was made from. That was unusual; she seemed to remember that there were laws about letting people know what was in cosmetics, so you didn't accidentally use something that you were allergic to.

So if there was no information on the label, how else might she be able to find out where this stuff came from and what was in it?

The Internet, of course. Shiny Time lip gloss probably had its own Web page.

She turned on her computer and opened the Web browser.

She clicked on her favorite search engine and typed in the name of the product.

Her cursor turned into an hourglass while the server searched the Internet, until it came up with a list of sites. There it was! Kelly clicked on the link for Shiny Time lip gloss and waited.

It took ages to load, and when it did, the page froze. Kelly couldn't access anything. Their Web site definitely hadn't been updated in quite a while. But it was so frustrating! How would Kelly ever learn more about the lip gloss?

She shrugged her shoulders as she picked up the jar.

"I'm sorry," she murmured aloud. "I really like using you, but no worthwhile company has such a bad Web site. And there've been too many awful coincidences. I can always get lip gloss that's just as nice from somewhere else."

She dropped the jar into her trash basket.

So much for her lucky lip gloss!

Kelly was in the bathroom brushing her teeth before bed later that evening. Looking at herself in the mirror, she remembered her promise to spend some time with Stacey. She had been so absorbed by the play that she'd totally forgotten about it. She frowned at herself.

"You're a bad sister," she said aloud.

She finished up in the bathroom and headed back to her own room to get into her pajamas before a final trip downstairs to say good night to her mom and dad.

She opened her bedroom door — and found Stacey going through her trash basket. It was an especially bizarre habit of hers.

"Hey! Excuse me," Kelly said. "Don't we have a rule about going into each other's bedrooms uninvited?" Stacey frowned at her. "I'm sorry I forgot you," Kelly said, "but we can't do anything together now. You should have been in bed two hours ago."

Stacy stood up and looked at her. "I'm sleep-walking!" she said. "I can't help myself."

Kelly smiled. "Well, sleepwalk out of here and go to bed before Mom catches you," she said. Stacey moved toward the door. "Hey, Stacey?" Kelly said. "Listen, we can play something tomorrow, as soon as I get back from school. How's that?"

"No problem," Stacey said.

That was odd. Normally she'd have heard a snotty response from Stacey. Then Kelly noticed that her sister was keeping one hand hidden behind her back as she walked past. And she seemed to be speed-walking out of the bedroom, as if she couldn't get out fast enough.

"Wait a minute," Kelly said, grabbing Stacey by her pajama sleeve. "What have you got in your hand?"

"Four fingers and a thumb," Stacey replied. "Let go of me."

"Not until I see what you've got there," Kelly insisted. She grabbed hold of the arm that Stacey was holding behind her and slowly twisted it around until her sister's hand was revealed. She was clutching the jar of lip gloss.

"What are you doing with that?" Kelly said.

"What do you care?" Stacey said. "You threw it away."

"You can't just come in here when you feel like it and take my stuff, even if it is in the trash," Kelly said. "What are you — a junior bag lady?" She plucked the jar out of Stacey's hand and let go of her.

"I hate you!" Stacey spat.

"I'll just have to try and live with that," Kelly said, shoving her out through the door. "Now just be a good little brat and *get lost!*"

She shut the door in Stacey's face.

There was an angry thump on the outside of the door.

Their mother's voice called up from downstairs. "What's going on up there? Stacey — are you out of bed?"

Kelly heard a scamper of feet across the landing and the soft click of Stacey's bedroom door closing.

"Little pest!" Kelly muttered. She went over to her bed to get her pajamas out from under the pillow.

On the way, she tossed the lip gloss back into the trash.

In the morning, she decided, she'd ask if she could have a lock put on her door. The way Stacey was behaving these days, that would be the only way to keep the irritating little monster out of her things.

Kelly was woken by the sound of running feet and subdued urgent voices on the landing outside her room. She didn't know why, but it made her sit up straight in bed, craning to listen harder. Was something bad happening?

She glanced at her bedside clock. It was 7:03.

Her alarm was set for half past seven. Quite often her parents were up earlier than that — but this was different. She didn't know how — but this was very different.

Her door opened a crack.

"Stacey? Are you in there?" came her mother's voice.

Kelly was wide awake now. "Mom?"

"Is Stacey in there with you?" her mom asked.

"No." Kelly shook her head. "What's wrong?"

"We can't find Stacey anywhere," her mom said. "And the front door's wide open."

A cold fear clenched in Kelly's stomach. She stumbled out of bed and ran across the room.

Now she could hear her father's voice calling from the street. "Stacey! Sta-ce-e-ey!"

Her mother ran down the stairs, fear etched on her face.

Kelly went straight to Stacey's room. She'd be hiding. Playing a stupid game.

The bedcovers were rumpled. Her pajamas, nightgown, and slippers were missing.

"Stacey — this isn't funny," Kelly said loudly, her voice trembling. "Come out right now."

Nothing.

She fell to her knees and looked under the bed. She squeezed in between the dresser and the wall to check that the skinny little girl wasn't hiding there. Then she pulled open the closet door and dragged out the mess of clothes and toys that filled the bottom.

There was no sign of Stacey.

Her own words rang out darkly in her mind.

Now just be a good little brat and get lost!

GET LOST!

She touched her fingers to her lips. There was still just the faintest trace of the lip gloss on them.

No! That was crazy.

It was impossible.

And yet . . .

She ran out of her sister's bedroom, searching frantically through all the upstairs rooms, desperate to find her — desperate to prove that Stacey's disappearance *wasn't her fault.*

She didn't find Stacey anywhere.

She arrived at the head of the stairs, feeling dizzy and sick.

She could hear her mother's voice on the phone. "Please come quickly. No. She's never done anything like this before. Thank you. Thank you."

Kelly sat heavily on the top step, staring down blankly at the open front door. She scraped her pajama sleeve hard across her lips, hurting her mouth, wiping off that last deadly remnant of lip gloss.

Her mother appeared at the bottom of the stairs.

"I've called the police," she said. "They're sending somebody over. They're going to start searching for her." She gave Kelly a brave smile. "They'll find her in no time," she said.

"It's my fault," Kelly said.

Her mother stared at her.

Tears spilled down Kelly's cheeks. "I told her to get lost," she said.

Her mother ran up the stairs and gathered Kelly in her arms.

"Don't be so silly," she said. "Of course it's not your fault."

"It is!" Kelly mumbled, her face buried in her mother's shoulder. "You don't understand."

"Yes, I do," her mother said. "You yelled at her, and she's gone off somewhere to frighten you and to pay you back." Kelly's mom took Kelly's face between her hands. "That's *good*, Kelly. That's good. That means she's OK — don't you see? She's done it to spite you. Don't worry — she couldn't have gone far. We'll find her soon."

Kelly wasn't so sure. "It's the lip gloss," she said. "The lip gloss made her get lost."

Her mother shook her head. "It doesn't matter what you had the fight over," she said. "Listen — get yourself washed and dressed. I'm going to tell your dad what happened." She ran back down the stairs.

Kelly wiped her eyes.

Completely numb, she rose to her feet and walked into the bathroom.

She looked at herself in the mirror. Her face was pale and drawn, and the fear in her eyes shocked her. She turned on the faucet and splashed cold water into her face.

Maybe her mom was right. Maybe Stacey had run off on purpose to teach Kelly a lesson. It wouldn't exactly be out of character for her to do something like that. Stacey could be extremely thoughtless at times, and she was capable of holding grudges for days on end. And a childish grudge was simply more likely than evil lip gloss.

Kelly went down to the front door. Her father was nowhere to be seen, but her mother was standing at the gate, looking down the street.

"I'll help look," Kelly called.

Her mother hurried back along the front path. "No," she said. "I want you to put on your school clothes. I'll make you some breakfast. Your dad will find Stacey. And the police will be here soon. Won't your sister love that?" she said, smiling grimly. "Causing all this disruption." Kelly could tell that her mother was try-ing to make it sound like everything would be all right — but Kelly could still hear the tremble in her voice.

"Let me help," Kelly said gently.

"No," her mother said. "If Stacey's hiding to punish you for yelling at her, then she might not come out if she hears your voice. You know how stubborn she can be." She guided Kelly to the bottom of the stairs. "Now, go up to your room and get dressed. I'll make you something to eat — then you can go to school just like you always do."

Kelly stared at her. "I can't just go to school like nothing's happened," she said in disbelief.

"Yes, you can," her mother said. "There's no point in you staying home. And I promise we'll call the school the moment she turns up." She looked into Kelly's face. "Everything will be fine, OK? Everything will be absolutely fine."

Kelly didn't want to go to school. She knew she wouldn't be able to concentrate on anything. But her mother insisted. She arrived at school in a daze of worry, just as the bell was ringing for homeroom. Part of her wanted to run around telling everyone what had happened — but after she thought about it some more, she decided to keep everything to herself. *If I don't mention Stacey's disappearance out loud*, she thought, *then maybe it won't be real.*

The world became very small as Kelly sat in her first

class. She couldn't stop turning to look at the wall clock at the back of the classroom. She couldn't believe how the minutes dragged — and still there was no news. The teacher's voice was just so much background noise. All Kelly could think about were the last words she had spoken to Stacey.

Get lost! GET LOST!

What if Stacey was never found? What if Kelly had to live the rest of her life without ever being able to tell Stacey she was sorry?

"Kelly!"

She stared blankly out of the window — seeing nothing, trapped in the never-ending nightmare of her thoughts.

"Kelly!"

The girl sitting next to her nudged her, and she came back into the real world with a start. Everyone was looking at her. Mrs. Kline, the principal's secretary, was standing next to the teacher at the front of the class.

"Kelly — there is an urgent telephone call for you," Mr. Wise said. "Go with Mrs. Kline now, please."

Kelly felt strangely numb now that the moment had come. Would the news be good? Or would it be . . .

No! Don't even think about that!

She scrambled up from her desk and followed Mrs. Kline out of the classroom.

"Is it about Stacey?" she asked anxiously. "Have they found her?"

Mrs. Kline smiled at her. "Yes, it does concern your sister," she said. "And, yes — I believe she has been found safe."

Kelly let out a gasp of relief, and the darkness that had been piling up inside her head fell away.

She ran into Mrs. Kline's office and scooped up the telephone receiver.

"Mom?"

"Yes, it's me, honey," came her mother's voice, flooded with relief. "We've found her!"

Kelly felt light-headed. Her legs buckled under her, and she sat down heavily, shaking uncontrollably and with tears of relief flooding down her face.

"Is she all right?" she managed to murmur into the phone.

"She's fine," said her mother. "She's muddy and con-fused and exhausted — but as far as we can tell, there's nothing wrong with her. I've put her to bed. The doc-tor is going to stop by later to take a quick look — just to be on the safe side."

"Where was she?" Kelly gasped. She noticed that she was gripping the receiver so tightly that her knuck-les were white. "What was she doing?"

"The police found her wandering around in a park on the other side of town," said her mother. "Lord only knows how she got that far — it must be a mile away. She was very confused when we got her home. She says she doesn't know how she got there."

"So she didn't run away to get back at me," Kelly said.

"I really don't think so," said her mother. "She seems like she genuinely doesn't know what happened to her. Your father thinks she may have simply sleep-walked out of the house, but at the moment, we don't know what happened. The important thing is she's back home, and everything's OK."

"I'll come home," Kelly said, suddenly desperate to see with her own eyes that Stacey was safe.

"No, there's no need for that. Everything's fine. She's sleeping now. You can see her this afternoon. You go back to your classes, Kelly."

"OK. If you're sure."

"I'm sure. Cheer up, honey — it's all over. Take care."

"Bye." Kelly sat there with the receiver in her hand. Mrs. Kline gently took it from her and replaced it on the phone's cradle. Then she handed Kelly some tissues to wipe her eyes.

She smiled at Kelly. "Sisters!" she said. "They can drive you out of your mind, can't they?"

Kelly looked at her. "She does sometimes," she admitted. "But she's great, really."

"Of course she is," Mrs. Kline said. "Are you feeling OK, or would you like to sit here quietly for a while?"

"No, I'm fine."

"Off you go, then."

Kelly headed back to her class.

It was all over.

Everything was fine.

The relief was overwhelming.

Kelly sat through the rest of the class in an exhausted daze. It was a good thing Mr. Wise didn't ask her any questions. She didn't have the faintest idea what he was talking about.

But as the immediate sensation of relief began to fade, it was replaced by other thoughts. Uncomfortable thoughts.

If Stacey had not run away on purpose, then what had really happened to her? Was Dad right — had she sleepwalked out of the house in the middle of the night and made her way halfway across town to the park? Why would that happen? She had never sleepwalked before — and why should she do it on the same night that Kelly told her to get lost?

Kelly touched her fingertips to her lips. There was nothing on them now — she had made sure of that. But there had been traces of the lip gloss on her lips last night when she had argued with Stacey.

Could it really be a coincidence?

Kelly reviewed the facts in her mind.

Her mother's bitten tongue. Fiona Oslow's broken leg. Tanya Barker's concussion. Nicole's tonsillitis. Stacey's disappearance.

All those things had happened following comments made by Kelly while she had been wearing the lip gloss.

And there was another thing. That weird store in the mall. There one day — gone the next. And the clerk in the place next door had said the space had been empty for months.

Shiny Time.

I know how crazy it sounds, Kelly said to herself, *but there's something bad about that lip gloss. I know there is.*

She thought of the little jar lying in her trash basket back at home. She had to get rid of it once and for all. She had to get it out of the house.

At the end of the class, she slipped quietly away from the stream of students moving up and down the hallways. Thank goodness Nicole hadn't returned to school yet — there was no one to ask awkward questions. Kelly hid by the lockers until everything was quiet, then exited through one of the side entrances. She ran across the athletic field and squeezed through a small gap in the chain-link fence. It was the traditional way of getting in and out of school when you didn't want to be seen.

She walked at normal speed along the street while she was still in sight of the school. If she was spotted, she had her alibi ready. A dental appointment.

Her heart was thundering as she approached the end of the street. Once she was around the corner and out of sight of the school, she should be safe.

She turned the corner, letting out a long, pent-up breath.

She began to run, the wind whipping through her hair as she raced along the sidewalk, desperate to get home as quickly as possible.

Desperate to get that horrible and dangerous lip gloss out of her home.

Everything looked strangely normal at the house. Kelly paused on the opposite sidewalk to catch her breath and wait for her pounding heart to slow down. She knew she had to get into the house and up to her room without being seen by her parents. They'd send her right back to school. They wouldn't understand about the lip gloss.

After all — who in their right mind would?

Once she had recovered, Kelly crossed the street and slipped down the side of the house. She was counting on the back door being unlocked.

It was. She slid silently into the kitchen, listening intently.

She could hear murmuring voices from the living room. Her mom and dad, talking softly together. She tiptoed quietly along the hall and crept up the stairs.

She paused on the landing, hardly daring to breathe. Stacey's bedroom door was open a crack — not enough for Kelly to see her sister, although she assumed she'd be tucked away in bed, fast asleep after her terrible ordeal.

As she crept past Stacey's door, Kelly shuddered as she thought of what might have happened to her little sister. She resolved to do something extra-nice for her once this was all over. Something that Stacey would really like.

She slowly and cautiously opened her own bedroom

door, listening intently for any sound of movement from downstairs.

She tiptoed across to her desk and crouched by the trash basket. She rummaged through the scraps and shreds of crumpled-up paper and tissues and other stuff she had thrown away.

The little jar of lip gloss wasn't anywhere obvious. She assumed it must have fallen straight to the bottom. She leaned over, digging through the things, feeling for the glass jar.

Nothing!

This was ridiculous. It had to be there.

Losing patience, she tipped over the trash basket and let the contents spill out onto her carpet. She sifted through the garbage.

Kelly heard a soft creak behind her, and her hands froze in midair.

She turned.

Stacey was standing in the doorway, dressed in her pajamas.

"Looking for this?" she said, in an icy voice.

She held up her hand — and between her fingers was the jar of lip gloss.

Kelly's heart skipped a beat, and a new panic shot through her like a bolt of electricity.

"Stacey," she said in a low, urgent voice. "Give me that, please."

The little girl glared defiantly at her. "Why should I? You threw it away."

"I know," Kelly said gently. "But it's dangerous. Trust me — give it to me." She reached out a hand toward her sister.

Stacey put her hand behind her back. "No way!" she said. "It's mine now — finders keepers!" She gave Kelly a big triumphant smirk — and that was when Kelly became aware of something new.

Stacey's lips were bright and shiny with a thick smear of lip gloss.

A cold dread filled Kelly.

"Stacey — please — don't say anything," she begged, rising to her feet and moving toward her sister. "Don't say a word. Just give me the jar. Please give me the jar."

Stacey gave her a contemptuous look. "Yeah — right!" she scoffed. "As if!" She turned and walked out onto the landing. "You know what you can do, Kelly?"

she said as she marched determinedly back to her room. "You can just . . . get . . . *lost!*"

Kelly was stunned by what her sister had said.

She stumbled out into the hall. "No! Stacey — no!" she called wildly. "Take it back! Please, take it back!" She gave a gasp as she felt a strange tingling sensation in her arms and legs.

"Brat!" came Stacey's voice, as if from far away.

A terrible certainty filled Kelly's mind. It really *was* the lip gloss — all along, it was the lip gloss that had caused all those dreadful things to happen. And now the curse had fallen on her.

She couldn't even cry out. It suddenly felt as if her heart and lungs were slowing to a pause.

She looked at her arms and then, shockingly, she found herself looking right *through* her arms. She was disappearing!

Kelly dropped to her knees, but her body somehow sank even farther than the floor would seem to permit. Confused and alone, she braced herself for what might happen next. She didn't know where or when she might reappear next.

If she was to reappear at all . . .